ADRIFT IN THE NOÖSPHERE

Borgo Press Books by DAMIEN BRODERICK

Adrift in the Noösphere: Science Fiction Stories
Chained to the Alien: The Best of ASFR: Australian SF Review
 (Second Series) [Editor]
Climbing Mount Implausible: The Evolution of a Science
 Fiction Writer
Embarrass My Dog: The Way We Were, the Things We Thought
Ferocious Minds: Polymathy and the New Enlightenment
Human's Burden: A Science Fiction Novel (with Rory Barnes)
I'm Dying Here: A Comedy of Bad Manners (with Rory Barnes)
Post Mortal Syndrome: A Science Fiction Novel (with Barbara
 Lamar)
Skiffy and Mimesis: More Best of ASFR: Australian SF Review
 (Second Series) [Editor]
Unleashing the Strange: Twenty-First Century Science Fiction
 Literature
Warriors of the Tao: The Best of Science Fiction: A Review of
 Speculative Literature [Editor with Van Ikin]
x, y, z, t: Dimensions of Science Fiction
Zones: A Science Fiction Novel (with Rory Barnes)

ADRIFT IN THE NOÖSPHERE

SCIENCE FICTION STORIES

DAMIEN BRODERICK

with Barbara Lamar and Paul Di Filippo

THE BORGO PRESS
MMXII

ADRIFT IN THE NOÖSPHERE

FIRST EDITION

Published by Wildside Press LLC

www.wildsidebooks.com

DEDICATION

For Barbara Lamar and Paul Di Filippo,
Apex Collaborators

CONTENTS

FOREWORD

BY RICH HORTON

I have to admit that until several years ago I didn't really know Damien Broderick's work. I was aware of it (as Martin says of Ray Bradbury in a Simpsons episode). I knew that novels like *The Dreaming Dragons* (aka *The Dreaming*—and don't forget that "aka"—Broderick is an inveterate improver of his earlier work) and *The White Abacus* were held in high regard. I knew he had a reputation as a critic as well as a writer. I knew he was Australian. That was about it.

My loss. Things began to change when I read for review his diptych *Godplayers* (2005) and *K-Machines* (2006), wild post-Singularity sf with echoes of Zelazny and Leiber, and akin to Charles Stross's *Accelerando* (2005) which drew upon the same extropian speculations surveyed in Broderick's 1997 *The Spike*. These are fast-moving and highly entertaining novels, deeply steeped in the field (and as such highly allusive), also deeply informed by exotic scientific speculation. And still fun! Along the way I also read Broderick's first novel, *Sorcerer's World* (1970), which nods at Vance, and has its moments but is perhaps a bit too much a young man's jape. (It, too, was significantly revised and extended in 1986 as *The Black Grail*.)

I also noticed Broderick's impressive achievements as a critic, evidenced by books like *Transrealist Fiction: Writing in the Slipstream of Science*, *Reading by Starlight: Postmodern Science Fiction*; and *x, y, z, t: Dimensions of Science Fiction*. In addition he has produced some impressive futurist-oriented popular science work, most notably *The Spike*. When I finally "met" Damien on a couple of online fora, I saw immediately a highly intelligent person, clever, sometimes sardonic, and (perhaps most important!) often sharing my tastes in sf.

But, you know, I tend to approach the field first through short fiction. And in 2009 Damien Broderick began to produce a not yet abated flood of quite remarkable shorter work, beginning with "Uncle Bones" and including such quite outstanding stories as "This Wind Blowing, and This Tide," "The Qualia Engine," and two included in this book: "Under the Moons of Venus" and "The Beancounter's Cat". These stories hooked me, no doubt about it.

One feature of Broderick's work, already hinted at, is the allusiveness towards earlier sf (or not necessarily sf: *The White Abacus*, for instance, is a science fictional version of *Hamlet*). This can be a dangerous thing—one can't depend on the reader to get one's allusions, to recognize who's being pastiched or even parodied. But Broderick succeeds in walking the tightrope (stretched, I suppose, over the Scylla and Charybdis of reader frustration at missing things and reader annoyance at traducing beloved past works) between providing a fully successful story on its own terms and at the same time deepening both the new story and the work alluded to by the embedded commentary and references. These new stories notably echo writers like Philip K. Dick, Cordwainer Smith, and J. G. Ballard, while throwing in the odd reference to Sturgeon, Kipling and Wilmar Shiras. But they, I think, will delight new readers as well.

This is the latest of several illuminating story collections. Each tends to combine early work (sometimes very early) with new stories (sometimes brand new, as with "Luminous Fish" in this book). I've been delighted to be able to follow the evolution of Broderick's work—for example, his very first story, "The Sea's Furthest End," which first appeared in 1964 in the first issue of Ted Carnell's classic UK original anthology *New Writings in SF*, is available in *Climbing Mount Implausible* in its original form; and in drastically revised form as "The Game of Stars and Souls" in *Uncle Bones*. (A still different version is the 1993 YA novel also called *The Sea's Furthest End*.) By all means read them both (or all three!)—the first version is indeed the work of a teenager, and shows it, but retains a distinct and refreshing energy, which manages to survive the later improvements. And from the beginning we can see the shape of the mature writer's interests. Even better is the chance to resurrect unjustly neglected stories, such as "The Ballad of Bowsprit Bear's Stead" (1980), which I first read in *Uncle Bones,* and which despite being thirty years old is one of my favorite novelettes in my recent reading. (I should have noticed it in 1980, but what can I say? I was a junior in college, and I missed a lot of stuff in favor of girls, beer, and physics.)

But what of the stories included here? They are a varied bunch, both in time of publication and theme. But every one is worth reading. There is a brand new story, "Luminous Fish," written with Paul Di Filippo, taking on Michael Moorcock's Jerry Cornelius character with stabs at sleazy websites and a Heinlein-like brain transplant. There are four first rate stories from the past couple of years: "Time Considered as a Series of Thermite Burns in No Particular Order," a clever and very funny time travel romp (with a serious aspect); "The Beancounter's Cat," set in a far future with Clarkean science sufficiently advanced to appear magic, and meditating on human destiny very effectively (on first reviewing this I called Broderick "one of our prophets of the posthuman"); "Walls of Flesh, Bars of Bone" (written with Broderick's wife, Barbara Lamar), is another look at the mystery of human destiny, beginning with an academic seeing himself in a film from 1931, and solving that mystery quite strangely; and finally one of the very best sf short stories of the past couple of years, "Under the Moons of Venus," which is either about what it purports to be: a man left nearly alone on an empty Earth after aliens take most people to Venus, or about a man gone mad—either way, it's remarkable, evocative, effectively in homage to one of sf's greats but still through and through original.

And there are the older stories. "All My Yesterdays" is one of his first stories, from 1964 (though slightly revised), and it's not bad at all, a day in the very long life of an evidently immortal man, battling with God. "Coming Back" is a mid-career story, a solid take on the story of a man stuck in a time loop. "The Womb" is a long story on the subject of UFOs and Ufologists and cults, intriguing odd stuff. And "All Summer Long" looks at intelligent robots and asks "What would they really want to do?"

Damien Broderick is one of our best contemporary writers of sf, and his recent spate of excellent short fiction, matched with excellent collections such as this, gives all of us a chance to discover this.

INTRODUCTION

BY DAMIEN BRODERICK

Seven years before I was born, far away and long ago, a British technology whiz who called himself "Professor" A.M. Low published a truly terrible novel for young readers titled *Adrift in the Stratosphere*. That was a couple of years before the fabled Golden Age of science fiction was kick-started by editor John W. Campbell, Jr., in the pages of a US magazine with the even pulpier title *Astounding Science Fiction*. Crude as that magazine's title was—and Campbell tried for years to change it to a simple *Science Fiction*, which would have helped a lot, and finally managed to shift it to *Analog*, still its name—a fresh spirit moved over what were already the rather stagnant waters of early sf.

Archibald Low missed out on these developments, alas, so his young Stratospheric adventurers followed the same ridiculous path to glory in space that had been hacked from the pulp jungle for many years. To quote the wry and entertaining summary by British wit David Langford,

> [Three young men] accidentally launch a "rocket-balloon" spacecraft left unattended by the professor who built it. Soon they're "passing through a belt of X-rays," causing the ship and their own bodies to become transparent. Next they dodge a living, mile-long air monster that flies at 800 mph.... Our heroes are tormented by yellow radium beams from Mars. Will they

discover the ship's anti-radium ray? [At length] they plunge to an emergency landing on a Fortean skyborne island.[1]

Surprisingly, in the year I was born, Low became, Langford reports, "the first-ever author named as a British sf convention's official guest." Surely it wasn't for *Adrift in the Stratosphere*.

I mention this grisly history because a couple of decades after its publication, I had contracted the sf infection, and haunted the closest library, several miles away by bike. I swiftly devoured all the regular science fiction in the place, and finally fetched up at "Professor" Low's weird emanation. I forced it down, gagging gently. A rocket-powered balloon! War with Martians via radio! (In a way, perhaps this had been a perceptive glimpse, in the mid-1930s, into Hitler's dreadfully effective use of the new mass media.) It was very silly, and yet, strangely, the title has stuck in my mind through all the decades since.

This was science fiction, but not as we know it, Jim.

§

And what of the Noösphere? Why, that was a notion I encountered at the start of the 1960s, long before people started wearing strange clothes and flowers in their hair. It was first proposed, though not named, by the Russian Vladimir Ivanovich Vernadsky (1863-1945), a founder of the discipline of geochemistry, whose book *The Biosphere* (1926) argued that our world has been shaped by the life swarming its surface, waters and air for billions of years. It was a forerunner of James Lovelock's idea of Gaia, but Vernadsky pushed it further: the planet's history had seen three mighty epochs, with the new realm of mind following those of inanimate and then living matter. This mental world, the Noösphere, is today given literal expression in the global skein of billions of messages flung through space,

---

1. http://www.sfsite.com/fsf/2008/cur0808.htm

wires, and cables, tying humankind into a kind of emerging hive mind.

The term was the coinage of a French Jesuit, Father Pierre Teilhard de Chardin, S.J. (1881-1955). Teilhard was a paleontologist and early supporter of evolutionary explanations for the shape of species and the biosphere—a somewhat risky proposition for a Catholic priest to maintain in the 1920s, when Darwin's *On the Origin of Species* remained on the *Index Librorum Prohibitorum*. Curiously enough, Teilhard's approach to the topic rejected Darwin's idea of gradual change via natural selection of random inherited characteristics. He was convinced that life's evolution is goal-directed, presumably following a path prescribed in advance by a divine Creator. The Noösphere, then, was the gradual fulfillment of this project at its highest levels, with the minds of humankind being drawn together into a gestalt unity that would become, at its highest or Omega Point, the veritable consciousness of Christ on Earth.

For a while, I thought this was a pretty cool idea. It resonated with a lot of feel-good tropes in science fiction, which tends to be godless yet mystical, non- or even anti-religious yet spiritual, anchored in scientific empiricism as an ideal method yet profoundly touched by a yearning for transcendence. The celebrated "sense of wonder" is its ensign. Eventually I learned enough about evolutionary biology and philosophy to realize that Teilhard de Chardin was, in effect, barking mad; his theories (or "theories") of *radial* and *tangential* energies were pure moonshine. It made as much sense as a rocket-propelled balloon into space. But wait—

As *metaphor* the Noösphere promised to be fertile!

Especially as a science fiction metaphor—one that applied to the stories themselves, as they clawed their way into existence in the heads of their authors and flourished into fresh life every time they entered the hungry consciousness of readers and viewers.

Humans are creatures of self-aware purpose (some of the time, anyway), utterly unlike the evolutionary process that cobbled us together. But we achieve our purposes as much by dreaming and playing games with ideas and imagined feelings as we do through deliberation and planning, or by following a path already set for us.

If sf is about anything, it's that endless, ever-changing dream, that set of imaginary games we play, using the endlessly renewed toolbox of the genre.

We're adrift, like voyagers on a raft, carried into strange seas by currents we can barely identify—adrift, indeed, in the Noösphere!

§

Some of my own voyages in the Noösphere, brief or extended, are gathered in this collection. Here's how they came into existence, and the wanderings that led me toward them.

"Time Considered as a Series of Thermite Burns in No Particular Order," to my delighted astonishment, was purchased the very afternoon I submitted it to Patrick Nielsen Hayden, at Tor.com, in 2011. It was my second sale to that website, and the story was elegantly illustrated by Victo Ngai. I hope it's funny, in a grim sort of way. One of these days I should get back to this time-traveling couple; I like them.

I've read a lot of robot stories in the last half century, most memorably Isaac Asimov's tales of his "positronic" humanoids, and John Sladek's sarcastic rejoinders snapping at their heels. But in all this trove of mechanical men, Terminators, robots stunned and led astray by paradox, there aren't many stories where robots...*just wanna have fun in the sun.* "All Summer Long " was commissioned by Australian editors Paul Collins and Meredith Costain, and telling it from the point of view of a kid seemed just perfect.

Some years ago, I produced a burst of stories one after the other without pause, a return to the short form after years of writing mostly novels and other books—although for five years I was sf editor of the Aussie popular science magazine *Cosmos,* which meant I was *reading* a lot of short fiction. Let me assure you, this is an experience guaranteed to engender sympathy with the lot of the editor. I was going great guns until I got to the opening stanzas of "The Beancounter's Cat," which I carelessly showed to a senior and very astute editor. He told me just what was wrong with it, and that killed me stone dead in mid-stream. I immediately lost the capacity to write short fiction. Trust me, this happens to more writers than you'd suppose (it hamstrung the great Theodore Sturgeon repeatedly). Some years later, the brilliant Australian editor Jonathan Strahan asked me if I could urgently send him something for his non-themed anthology *Eclipse Four*. Why yes, of course, I said, and pulled out my false start. I saw quickly where I'd been going wrong, and had a very pleasant time reinventing the direction of the story, no longer adrift. It appeared from Nightshade Books in 2011, and I was charmed when Gardner Dozois took it for his 2012 Year's Best SF volume.

Gardner had already bought reprint rights to "Under the Moons of Venus" for the 2011 Year's Best SF anthology—and so too had the editors of four other Year's Bests (David Hartwell and Kathryn Cramer, Rich Horton, Allan Kaster, and Jonathan Strahan). I was startled to find how few other sf stories have been snapped up by so many different anthologies in a single year, and heartened by the success of this ambiguous tale. Is the protagonist psychotic and delusional, or has the solar system been rewritten by Singularity-grade entities? You must be the judge, but I think it all really happened just the way it seems. This was another story bought by Jonathan Strahan, and appeared in *Subterranean*, in 2010. It was a finalist for the 2011 Sturgeon Award.

As I write this, I'm in the process of proofreading a book I wrote with Paul Di Filippo, *Science Fiction: The 101 Best Novels, 1985-2010*. That's an ambitious guide to the finest long fiction sf in the years after those surveyed in David Pringle's remarkable *Science Fiction: The 100 Best Novels, 1949-1984*. Paul and I have never met, but we're frequent contributors to the internet chat group Fictionmags. Our first story together was "Cockroach Love," in 2008. (It's in my 2010 book *Climbing Mount Implausible: The Evolution of a Science Fiction Writer*.) Our follow-up, "Luminous Fish," is a tribute to the confrontational Jerry Cornelius stories devised by Michael Moorcock and others, and appears here (with Mike's permission) for the first time.

Reading "Coming Back," from *F&SF* in 1982, is a bit like watching the 1993 Bill Murray movie *Groundhog Day* a number of times in a row. Sometimes people adrift in the Noösphere find themselves caught in a whirlpool, sucked into the same Sargasso of idea. I don't know who originated the notion in this story, but it wasn't Danny Rubin and Harold Ramis (although they came up with an excellent and very funny script). It wasn't sf veteran Richard Luphoff, whose 1973 story (in *F&SF* nine years before mine, although I've never read it) was also filmed for TV in 1993. Maybe it was me in 1971, when I published the original version of "Coming Back," as "All the Time in the World," under the jesting by-line Alan Harlison, in the Aussie men's magazine *Man*. But I wouldn't be surprised if the notion goes back to the Greeks, or further.

"Walls of Flesh, Bars of Bone" is another story commissioned by the indefatigable Jonathan Strahan, for his 2010 anthology *Engineering Infinity*. It is one of several collaborations by me and my wife Barbara Lamar. Our longest is a 400 page sf/ thriller, *Post Mortal Syndrome,* which was the first novel serialized on-line in Australia (by *Cosmos*, the beautiful popular science magazine) in 2005, and released by Borgo Press in trade paperback in 2011. Barbara and I met through mutual interest in advanced technology, especially the kinds associated with the prospect of extended healthy longevity; at the time, she lived on her permaculture farm in Texas, and I in suburban Melbourne, Australia, and we were quite literally brought together by a confluence in the Noösphere. Nowadays we live near downtown San Antonio in a heritage-listed dwelling, formerly the family seat of the Texan painters Robert Onderdonk and his impressionist son Julian. We don't, though, own an early Rauschenberg.

Just for the form of the thing, and for auld lang syne, let's dip back to the dawn of time for my 1964 story "All My Yesterdays," which I revised slightly for Van Ikin's anthology *Glass Reptile Breakout,* in 1990. Frankly, it's more a fantasy than sf, unless an interventionist deity (rather more annoying than Teilhard's) is regarded as an sf idea.

Finally, "The Womb" was one of the longest pieces in the landmark 1998 original anthology *Dreaming Down Under,* winner of the World Fantasy Award in 1999, edited by Jack Dann and Janeen Webb. Jack is my doppelgänger; he moved from the US to Australia after falling in love with writer, editor, and literary scholar Dr. Webb, and they spend most of their time there now, while I rusticate in the States. Meanwhile, the very much longer, closely detailed saga of Daimon Keith and his daughter Flake is told in the collaborative novel *Dark Gray,* by Rory Barnes and me, released in the US in 2010 by Fantastic Books.

§

All of these stories—all sf stories in general, perhaps all fiction—drift in the Noösphere, drawn and shoved by the currents of strange attractors we rarely identify. Perhaps science fiction is the story-telling medium best suited for this understanding. At its best, it is not programmatic, not goal-driven by ideology or compulsion (yet not, of course, plotless)—a kind of zestful or mournful or hilarious or yearning contemplation impelled by wonderment. These stories are my attempts upon that ambition.

It's appropriate, perhaps, to close with a few of the thoughts of Pierre Teilhard de Chardin, who taught that "Driven by the forces of love, the fragments of the world seek each other so that the world may come to being." But he wasn't always so high-toned. Sometimes the world bit him on the ass, as it does with us: "Growing old is like being increasingly penalized for a crime you haven't committed." But finally he and we know this much: "It is our duty as men and women to proceed as though the limits of our abilities do not exist." And who knows— maybe those abilities, enhanced by deepening knowledge, will burgeon and continue to enrich and enliven us, as our favorite fiction promises. Meanwhile, here are the stories.

TIME CONSIDERED AS A SERIES OF THERMITE BURNS IN NO PARTICULAR ORDER

My time machine was disguised as a Baronne Henriette de Snoy rosebush in full bloom. I left it in the Royal Botanic Gardens, next to a thicket of imported English foliage. We could have appeared near the Library building itself, but I wanted to get the lay of the land and insinuate myself. Besides, seeing time machines pop out of the air can make people nervous. Moira remained inside, shielded, and said through my inload, "Good luck, Bobby. Try not to get arrested again."

"Should be back in a couple of hours, max," I murmured. The internet and global communications systems had been dismantled some six decades earlier, after the tsunami of leaked classified documents. "I'll keep the images rolling, but let's nix the chitchat. Oh, and if I do get arrested, maybe you should come and get me."

My wife sighed. "Just don't get all tangled up, I hate time loops."

There were still trams running along St. Kilda Road, so I waited at the nearest stop and took one up Swanston Street to the State Library.

In this year the trams floated atop some kind of monorail set flush into the road, probably a magnetic levitation effect. Luckily, as the garbled pre-catastrophe records suggested, public transport was free in 2073 Melbourne, so I had no hassles with out-of-date coins or lack of swipe cards or injected RFID chips, all that nonsense that's tripped me up before and always ruins a nice outing. Especially if it ends with incarceration in the local lockup.

On the tram, I had a different kind of hassle, the usual sort. Other passengers stared at me with surprise, disdain or derision. You couldn't blame them. For obvious reasons, we'd found no reliable records in 2099 or later of the fashions in 2073. I was clad in the nearest thing to a neutral garment Moira and I have ever come up with: an inconspicuous gray track suit, no hoodie, sports shoes (you never know when you're going to have to run like hell, and anyway they're comfortable unless you find yourself up to your ankles or knees in an urban Greenhouse swamp), backpack.

A broad-shouldered youth with acne was nudging his bald oafish associates and rolling his eyes in my direction. I moved further down the tram and tried to merge with the crowd. Most of the men, except a few elderly, sported shaved heads decorated with glowing shapes that moved around like fish in a bowl. The women wore their hair like Veronica Lake in those old 1940s black and white movies. We crossed Collins Street, which didn't look all that different from 1982 or 2002, it's startling how persistent the general look of a city can be even in periods of architectural enthusiasm and mad-dog greedy developers. The thug followed me toward the back, smirking. He grabbed my track suit pants from behind and tried to give me a wedgie. My pack got in his way. I had a neuronic whip in my pocket, an Iranian special I'd picked up at a flea market in 2034, and I wrapped my hand around it but didn't want to use it and cause a ruction.

"You're a bloody weird, dinger," the thug informed me. "Watcha, going to a fancy dress party with yer downpoot mates?" He jolted me with a knee to my thigh, and I oofed.

"Don't hurt him, Bobby," Moira hissed in my inload. "My dog, what the hell are these morons wearing?"

A seated middle-aged fellow was jostled and got to his feet.

"See here, enough of this lollygagging foof! Leave the poor fellow alone, it's obvious he's a braindrain." He took my arm, and stepped past me. "Here, son, have my seat. I'm getting out at Lonsdale anyway." He trod heavily on the thug's foot as he passed, confident in his shiny top hat. Probably didn't hurt much, they wore something like soft woolen gloves on their feet, each toe separately snug, and I hoped water repellent. Maybe the Greenhouse effect wasn't quite critical yet, but Melbourne is famous for its abrupt downpours.

"Lonsdale, yeah, me, too," I said, for Moira's benefit, and followed him closely, to the jeers of the style-conscious oafs. My thigh hurt, but I had to force myself not to smile. Obviously this was one of those tiresome years when almost everyone bowed to the dictates of fashion. I stepped down from the tram onto the traffic island, surveyed the citizens wandering along the street, young and old and in between, and despite myself burst out laughing anyway. It was like some kind of cosplay epidemic had overtaken downtown, maybe the whole continent. For a moment the attire had baffled me. It was baggy in the wrong places and tight everywhere else. Looked horribly uncomfortable, but that seems to be the rule with fashion in a lot of decades.

"Bobby, this is crazy!" Moira was laughing in my inner ear. "They're all wearing their pants over their heads!"

It wasn't just those on the tram. Most of the men in 2073 Melbourne central district, I realized with another snort of amusement, were wearing business suit trousers or blue jeans on top, arms through the rolled-up legs, sparkly shaven heads shoved through the open flies. A few women with their hair up in luxurious folds wore the same, although many preferred skirts, hanging down over their arms like something a nun would have worn back when I was a kid, in the days before nuns dressed like social workers.

"And check out the leggings," I muttered under my breath.

Everyone had their legs through the knitted arms of merrily

patterned sweaters, cinched at the waist by the inverted trouser belts. Something modestly blocked the neck holes. I saw after a moment that baseball caps were sewn into the necks, brims forward for the men, up or down depending on age, and backward for women, like tails. I could tell by the sniggers and glances that passers-by all despised my own absurd and out-of-date garb.

"Wow, fashion statement," Moira said.

"You think this is silly, check your wiki for eighteenth century toffs. Those stupid wigs. Those silk stockings. Gak." A woman gave me a sharp glance. Man in ridiculous clothes talking to himself in broad daylight, cell phones a thing of the past. "Hey, I'd better shut up and get it done."

I crossed to the Library at Little Lonsdale Street, settling my pack more comfortably. It was heavy on my shoulders. Item by item, we've worked out the optimal contents for the pack: obvious things, like food for several days, a sealed course of Cipro plus a box of heavy duty acetaminophen, two rolls of toilet paper (you'd be amazed and depressed how often that turns out to be a life saver), a code-locked wallet of cards and coins from several eras, although hardly ever the ones you need right now, but still, a googlefone that doesn't work beyond 2019 because they keep "upgrading" the "service" and then it stops, a Swiss Army knife of course, a set of lockpicks, a comb, a false beard and a cut-throat razor (useful for shaving and cutting throats, if it ever comes to that), and a holographic wiki I picked up in 2099 containing yottabytes of data on everything anyone will ever have learned about anything but with an index I still haven't mastered. One of these days. And that wiki might not even exist if I botched this job.

I paused on the Library steps, under the bold banners proudly announcing next week's unprecedented exhibition of the original Second Mars Expedition logs. No need to look again at a map of the floor plans, we'd got all those from water-stained future records and I'd memorized everything that seemed relevant. I rummaged, found my bottle of aluminum thermite powder and an upregulated ceramic cigarette lighter, put them carefully in separate pockets. The Optix woven into my hair was recording everything in its field of view, date-stamped for later archiving. If I got out of this alive and in one piece. At least Moira would have it backed up.

§

I left the backpack at the counter, where it was stored for me in a locked cabinet, but nobody patted me down to find the pocketed neuronic whip and my other handy tools or insisted that I pass through a scanner. That had been several decades earlier, when people were more angstish about everything. Still, I was sweating slightly. They'd removed most of the paper books from the library, except for displays of volumes set up as objets d'art, and the great circular reading room with its groaning wheeled chairs and hooded green lamps was full of chatter. People leaned across long tables toward each other, disputing like students in a yeshiva, displays flickering with information and gossip. Immersive learning, they'd called it back here in the 2070s—not a bad way of finding your way around the dataverse, and a damned sight more sensible than the droning memorization I'd had to put up with as a kid.

I found a librarian eventually and asked to speak to the Director of Collections. She looked at me with extreme distrust but put a call through and finally sent me across to an audience with Dr. Paulo Vermeer, who regarded me with similar sentiment. I tried not to stare at the Bessel function graphs dancing on his naked skull.

"Doctor, thank you for seeing me. I'm hoping that I might have the privilege of viewing the Second Mars Expedition logs in the vaults here, before they go on public display next week."

"And you are?"

"Professor Albert M. Chop," I told him, "Areologist," and presented a very sincere Fijian passport card with my holographic likeness rising from its embossed surface, a University of the South Pacific faculty ID, and a driver's license dated 2068. He gave them a perfunctory glance.

"You're young for such a post."

"It's a new discipline, of course." I wanted to tell him that I was older than he, just the lucky beneficiary of longevity plasmids from the end of the century. Instead, I watched as he regarded me with bland mockery.

"Whatever is that costume, Mr. Chop, and why are you wearing it in these hallowed halls?"

"It's my habit," I said, and tried to look humble but scholarly. Moira was sniggering again in my ear; I tried to ignore her and keep a straight face.

"Your what?"

"My religious garb, sir. Those of my faith, of a suitably elevated rank, are enjoined by the sacred—"

"What faith is that?" Perhaps it occurred to him that I might be affronted at an implied slur on my beliefs, and could bring him and the library up on charges. "Naturally we honor all forms of worship, but I have to admit that until now—"

"I am a Chronosophist," I said, and reached into my pocket. "Here, I have a fascinating display unit that will bring you enlightenment, Dr. Vermeer. Why, if you will set aside just one hour of your time—"

He gave a civilized, barely visible shudder. "No need for that, my good fellow. Very well, come along with me. But don't think—" and he sent me an arch look—"you can make a habit of it." I raised one eyebrow, something I'd trained myself to do as a kid when I was a big fan of Commander Spock. That was before real starflight, of course. As Vermeer slid out from behind his desk on a prosthesis, I saw that he'd lost both his legs, presumably in the Venezuelan conflict. Nothing I could do about that, alas. But I had larger fish to fry than a simple limited if brutal armed drone conflict. I followed him to a lift and we rose one floor. He let me into a humidity-controlled sealed room, and directed a functionary to open a vault. The Mars documents remained inside their triple-layer packaging. Even so, the

Director drew on a pair of long transparent gloves, fitting them snugly under the turn-ups of his trousers, and wrapped his nose and eyes in a white surgical mask. He handed me a medical kit. "Put these on. We can't risk damaging precious heirlooms with our breath and bodily aerosols."

I was already fitted out with antiviral plugs deep inside my nostrils, but I put on mask and gloves and watched in terror as he slid open the containers and placed them carefully on the table. I reached cautiously for the documents, and the Director blocked my hand.

"Strictly hands-off, Professor! Look but do not touch."

The functionary, a bored fellow some inches shorter and stouter than I, waited with his eyes out of focus, probably watching some Flix drivel. I took the neuronic whip out of my pocket and buzzed the Director to sleep. His head fell forward and hit the table. The functionary gave his boss an astonished look, but by that time I was beside him and cold-cocked him with the whip's butt. I kicked out of my KT-26 joggers, dragged off his clothes, struggled into them over my own, got my feet stuck in the arms of his numbered Demons football team sweater-trousers. I shoved, had them in place, tugged the shoes back on—I needed something sturdier than a pair of foot mittens. I heaved both men well clear, piled up a stoichiometric mixture of powdered iron oxide and aluminum, and set fire to it with the enhanced lighter. It went up with an explosive huff, and the hot blue blaze evaporated the death-laden logs and started to melt the top of the steel table.

The Director was stirring. I ran to the door, flung it wide. "Fire, fire!" I screamed, and ran to the elevator. "Quick, the treasures!" The polished cedar doors of the old lift creaked open. It was empty. Offices were opening, faces gaping. I flung myself in, hit the ground floor button, breathed deeply as the elevator descended, stepped forth slowly in a dignified manner, paused to retrieve my backpack. Shouts and bells broke out in earnest behind me.

As I skipped light-heartedly down the gray steps and onto

the grass, something fast and heavy slammed into my upper back, flung me forward on my face. I rolled, twisted, came up in a crouch, but the Director's prosthetic had pulled away out of reach. His face was livid with fury. I grabbed at my bruised neck. The rolls of toilet paper had saved me from having my spine ruptured, but I still felt as if I'd been kicked by a horse. Three fat guards tore down the steps, batons raised. I could have killed the lot of them, but my job here was to keep a low profile (ha!) and save lives. A lot of lives. Millions of lives. Mission accomplished.

I sighed and held my hands away from my body. It's a shame you can't loop back into your own immediate history or I'd have seen a dozen later versions of me popping up from the gathering crowd, coming to my rescue. Nope, it just didn't work that way. Maybe Moira—

Through gritted teeth, she was saying in my inload, "Damn it, Bobby, are you all right? Your vitals look okay. Hang on, I'll be with you in a—"

They hauled me inside again and this time the lift took us down into the basement.

"On my way," Moira told me. Then, in a softer tone, she said, "Bobby, honey, you done good. Real good. Nine million lives spared. Oh man. When I spring you, we are going to have a party, baby."

§

"You are the worst kind of terrorist," Director Vermeer told me in a chill, shaking voice. "In a matter of seconds you destroyed not lives but the very meaning of lives, the certified historical foundation that—"

"So the Martian logs are entirely destroyed?" I tried to rise; two overweight but chunky-muscled guards held me down. At least the functionary I'd stripped of his outer garments wasn't in the room. His pilfered clothing had been taken away and I suppose returned to him, or maybe held for some kind of forensic examination. I'd expected the place to be swarming with firefighters, ladders, gushing hoses, media cameras. No such thing. Evidently the vault room's internal fire protection systems had done the job, but not in time.

"Entirely incinerated, you barbarian."

"Thank dog for that!"

"And blasphemous mockery on top of this devastation, 'Professor' Chop." I could hear the inverted commas. "Oh yes, I wasted no time checking your absurd alibi. The University in Suva has no record of you, no faith exists called Chronosophy, nor is there any Albert M.—"

I chopped him off. "True. I had to deceive you to gain access to those festering Martian plague vectors. You have no idea how lucky you are, Director. How lucky the entire world is."

"What fresh nonsense is this?"

"In two days' time you'd have—" There was a knock at the door of the curator's office, a long narrow room decorated with holograms of flaring galaxies, rotating, peeling, multi-plying nucleic acids, two lions mating rather terrifyingly again and again in a loop, and other detritus of Installations and Exhibitions past. A woman with a floral skirt down to her wrists said apologetically, "Pardon me, Director, but there's a police Inspector here to speak to the, the prisoner."

My heart sank. I looked up gloomily, and Moira, in full police uniform worn upside down, but with a peaked cap covering her short red hair, said, "Good afternoon, Director. With your permission, I'd like to speak to this man in private for a moment. Then we'll be taking him across to Police Headquarters where he will be charged with this heinous offense." She was carrying my backpack.

"Very well, Inspector. I hope to hear a full accounting in due course. This arson is the most egregious—"

My wife shepherded him to the door, and shooed out the guards with him. "Please take a seat, Mr.... What should I call you?" she said for the sake of the Library staff milling on the other side of the closing door. It clicked shut.

"I think you could call me 'Bobby,' honey. Delighted to see you, but how do we proceed from here? We can't just stroll out and take a tram to the Botanic Gardens."

"The machine's out the back. No sense mucking around."

"Who did you clobber, by the way?"

"Some poor cow downstairs. Had to drag her into the loo to get her uniform off her. She's trussed up in one of their quaint cubicles. Someone's bound to find her, if you'll pardon the expression."

Moira was hyper, on the verge of babbling; she always gets that way when she's pulled off some amazing exploit.

"Okay, sweetie." I stood up, groaning, and she marched me toward the door in a stern and professional gait. "Lay on, MacDuff."

The lift took us back to the ground floor, where the director hovered, literally. "We have transport waiting at the back entrance," Moira told him. "Let's keep this as low profile as possible, no sense getting people hysterical. The brain drain is under sedation, he'll give me no trouble."

We made our way briskly through confusing corridors to the back, me giving a glazed fish eye to anyone we passed. There was no vehicle, of course, but the drab graveled back space was relieved by a handsome rosebush in a large wooden pot. Nobody was watching us. It's amazing what an air of authority and slight menace can do. We entered the disguised time machine and Moira, in the pilot's seat, took us forward a year. It was three in the morning when we emerged, so the place was deserted. But the city lights were bright in the crisp air, and from somewhere to the northeast we heard music and laughter. No plague. No epidemic of murderous nanomites from Mars. Another horrible future with its teeth pulled, made safe for humankind. Hooray, hooray.

"What's up, sweetie? Let's go back to 2099 and put our feet up." She started to snigger. "My dog, Bobby, you were a class act with your legs jammed into a sweater and your boof head sticking out of some guy's fly. Come on, what's up?"

"Candidly," I told her, feeling dreary, "I'm feeling dreary. How stale, flat and unprofitable are the uses of this world."

"Come on, buddy." My wife jabbed me in the ribs. She's just a little thing, but her elbow is sharp, even through a stolen blue police skirt. "Remember our motto, and be proud."

"A stitch in time," I said without much enthusiasm. It's the nature of our trade. You can change your future but not your own past. So you're obliged to go further and further into the day after the day after, and track down tomorrow's atrocities that can be reversed earlier in unborn histories you've never lived through, have no real stake in. Guardians of time, that's us. We can go home, sure, as far as our first time trip, but no further back than that. No way we can repair the horrors of our own past, the local history that made us: assassinations of the great and good, genocides, terrorist attacks, our own insignificant but painful goofs. It's like something from a Greek tragedy or myth, seems to me sometimes. Doomed to fix everyone else's atrocities and never get any thanks, and no chance to remedy our own mistakes.

But Moira was hugging me, and the sky was clear and filled with faint stars, through the light-spattered towers of Melbourne in 2074, which is more than could be said for some other epochs. So I hugged my wife back, and found myself grinning down at her. "Yeah. Okay. A stitch in time—"

"Saves nine," she said. "Nine million lives, this time. Maybe our own grand-grandkids, if we decide to. So hey, let's feel good about that, eh?"

"You bet." I said. I did feel better, a bit. "Party time it is, honey."

And we fell away into the future, again.

THE BEANCOUNTER'S CAT

A humble beancounter lived in Regio city near the middle of the world. Those of her credentials known outside the Sodality were modest but respectable. By dint of dedicated service and her particular gift, she had won herself a lowly but (she hoped) secure position with the Arxon's considerable staff of publicani. Still, on a certain summer's smorning, she carelessly allowed her heart to be seduced by the sight of a remarkable orange-furred cat, a rough but handsome bully of the back alleys. He stood outside her door, greeting the smallday in fine yodeling voice, claws stropped to a razor finish, whiskers proud like filaments of new brass.

"Here, puss," she called into the dusty lane.

The beancounter poured milk into a blue-rimmed bowl, inviting this cat inside the doorway of her little house, which was located in the noisy, scrofulous Leechcraft District. She watched the elegant animal lapping, and pressed the palms of her hands together in front of her modest but respectable breast.

"I believe I shall name you Ginger," she told the cat with considerable satisfaction.

The orange cat sat back and licked his whispers delicately, then bent to attend to his hindquarters, raising one leg. Holding the leg in the air he gave her a sour look.

"For Skydark's sake," said the cat, "must I abide this arrant sentimentality?" He nosed a little more, then lowered his leg and rose to all four feet, still bristling. "In any event, if you're interested, I already possess a name."

The beancounter had fallen upon her bottom, goggling at the loquacious and shockingly illegal animal.

"You can spea—" But she cut off the rest of the banal sentence that was about to escape her mouth, which she clamped shut. The cat gave her a sardonic glance and returned to the bowl, polishing off the last of the milk.

"Slightly rancid, but what else can you expect in this weather? Thank you," he added, and made for the door.

As the luminous tip of his tail vanished, the beancounter cried, "Then what is your name, sir?"

"Marmalade," the cat said, in a muffled tone. And then he was gone.

§

At the sleeping hour, she sat on piled cushions in a nook, peeling and eating slivers of a ripe golden maloon, and read to herself verses from a sentimental book, for she had nobody else to speak them to her. She read these tender verses by the guttering light of an oil-fruit lamp, the blood mounting in her cheeks. Secretly she knew it was all make-believe and artful compensation for a delayed life held pendant in her late mother's service, and she was ashamed and depressed by her fate. The beancounter was comely enough, but her profession stank in the nostrils of the general company. Suitable men approached her from time to time, in the tavern, perhaps, or at a concert, and expressed an initial interest in flattering terms. Every one of them swiftly recoiled in distaste when he learned of her trade. To a handsome poet she had tried an old justification: "It is a punishment, not a life-long deformity!" The fellow withdrew, refusing her hand.

She put the verses aside and brooded for several moments on the augmented beast. Had it been lurking all this time in the forests, mingling in plain sight with its witless kin of the alleys? It seemed impossible, unless its kind were more intelligent and devious than human people. Could it have fallen from above, from the dark heights above the Heights? Nothing of that kind had been bruited for thousands of years; she had always supposed such notions were the stuff of mythology, invented and retold generation after generation to frighten children and keep them obedient. Yet her mother's Sodality teachings verged on that conceit, if you stopped listening for allegory and metaphor and accepted her teachings at face value.

Bonida shuddered, and lay down on her bedding. Sleep would cure these phantasms.

§

The very next sday, the cat came back. The beancounter awoke, nostrils twitching. The brute had placed a pungent calling card on her doorstep. He sat with his back to her as she opened the door, and finally turned with a lordly demeanor and allowed her to invite him in. She put a small flat plate of offal on the floor next to her kitchen table. The animal sniffed, licked, looked up disdainfully.

"What is this muck?"

She regarded him silently, caught between irritation, amusement, and suppressed excitement. She detected no machine taint, yet surely this was a manifest or, less likely, the luckless victim of one, ensnared in the guise of a beast. She had waited all her life for such an encounter.

After a long moment, the cat added, "Just messin' wid you. Lighten up, woman." He bent his thickly furred orange head to the plate and gulped down his liver breakfast.

The beancounter broke her own fast with oaten pottage, sliced fruits and the last of the milk (it *was* going off, the cat was right) mixed in a beautifully glowing glazed bowl in radiant reds, with a streak of hot blue, from the kiln in the Crockmakers' Street. She spooned it up swiftly, plunged her bowl and the cat's emptied dish into a wooden pail of water, muttered the cantrip of a household execration, a device of the Sodality. The water hissed into steam, leaving the crockery cleansed but hot.

"Marmalade, if you're going to stay here—"

"Who said anything about staying?" the cat said sharply.

"If, I said. Or even if you mean to visit from time to time, I should introduce myself." She put out one small hand, fingers blue with ink stains. "I'm Bonida."

Marmalade consider the fingers, while scratching rapidly for a moment behind his ear. He replied before he was done with his scratch, and the words emerged in a curious burble, as if he were speaking while gargling. "I see. All right." Somewhat to her surprise, he stood, raised his right front paw with dignity and extended it. Her fingertips scarcely touched the paw before it was withdrawn, not hastily, but fast enough to keep Bonida in her place. She smiled secretly.

"You may sit on my lap if you wish," she told the cat, moving her legs aside from the table and smoothing her deep blue skirt.

"Surely you jest." The cat stalked away to investigate a hole in the wainscoting, returned, sat cattycorner from her and groomed diligently. Bonida waited for a time, pleased by the animal's vivid coat, then rose and made herself an infusion of herbs. "So," the cat said, with some indignation. "You make the offer, you snatch it away."

"Soon I must leave for my place of employment," she told him patiently. "If you are still here when I return, there will be a bowl of milk for you."

"And the lap?"

"You are always welcome on my lap, m'sieur," she said, and drank down her mug of wake-me-up, coughing hard several times.

"You'd certainly better not be thinking of locking me in!"

"I shall leave a window ajar," she told him, head reeling slightly from the stimulating beverage. She cleared her throat. "That's dangerous in this neighborhood, you know, but nothing is too good for you, my dear pussycat."

The cat scowled. "Sarcasm. I suppose that's preferable to foolish sentimental doting. I'll spare you the trouble." With an athletic spring, he was across the floor and at the door. "Perhaps

I'll see you this evening, Bonida Oustorn, so have some more of that guts ready for me." And was off, just the tip of his orange tail flirted at the jamb, curiously radiant in the dim ruby light of the Skydark.

Bonida stared thoughtfully. "So you knew my name all along," she murmured, fetching her bonnet. "Passing strange."

§

Above the great ramparts of the Heights, which themselves plunged upward for twenty-five kilometers, the Skydark was an immense contusion filling most of heaven, rimmed at the horizon by starry blackness. In half a greatday, forty sdays, Regio city would stand beneath another sky displaying blackness entire choked with bright star pinpoints, and a bruised globe half as wide as a man's hand at arm's length, with dull, tilting rings, a diminutive, teasing echo of the Skydark globe itself. Then the Skydark would be lost to sight until its return at dawn, when its faint glow would once again relentlessly drown out the stars, as if it were swallowing them.

These were mysteries beyond any hope of resolution. Others might yet prove more tractable.

The vivid, secret ambition of this woman, masked by an air of diffidence, was to answer just one question, the cornerstone of her late mother's cryptic teaching in the Sodality, and one implication of that answer, whatever it might be: What, precisely, was the nature of the ancient Skyfallen Heights; and from whence (and why) were they fallen? That obscurity was linked by hidden tradition, although in no obvious way, to the ancient allegory of Lalune, the Absent Goddess.

Certainly it had been no part of her speculations, entertained since late childhood, to venture that the key to the mystery might be a cat, one of the supposedly inarticulate creatures from lost Earth, skulking in this city positioned beside the world-girdling and all-but-impassable barrier of the Heights. Now the possibility occurred to her. It seemed too great a coincidence that the orange beast had insinuated himself into her dismal routine in the very week dedicated to the Sodality's summer Plenary. Marmalade had designs upon her.

With an effort, Bonida put these matters out of her mind, patiently showing her identity scars as she entered the guarded portico of the district Revenue Agency. As always, the ante-room to her small office, one of five off a hexagonal ring, stank with the sweat of the wretches awaiting their appointments. She avoided their resentful gaze, their eyes pleading or reddened with weeping and rage. At least nobody was howling at the moment. That would come soon enough. Seated at her desk, check-marking a document of assessment with her inky nib, she read the damning evidence against her first client. Enough pilfering to warrant a death sentence. Bonida closed her eyes, shook her head, sighed once, and called his name and her room number through the annunciator.

"You leave the Arxon no choice," she told the shaking peti-tioner. A powerfully built farmer from the marginal croplands along the rim of Cassini Regio, and slightly retarded, Bai Rong Bao had withheld the larger portion of his tax for the tenth part of a greatyear. Was the foolish fellow unaware of the records kept by the bureaucracy, the zeal with which these infractions were pursued and punished? Perhaps not unaware, but somehow capable of suppressing the bleak knowledge of his eventual fate. As, really, were they all, if the doctrines of the Sodality were justified true knowledge, as her mother had insisted.

"I just need more time to pay," the man was blubbering.

"Yes, farmer Bai, you will indeed pay every pfennig owed. But you have attempted very foolishly to deceive our masters, and you know the penalty for that. One distal phalange." Her hand was tingling. Her loathing for the task was almost unen-durable, but it was her duty to endure it.

"Phal—What's that?" He clutched his hands desperately behind his back. "They say you tear off a hand or a foot. Oh, please, good mistress, I beg you, leave me whole. I will pay! In time. But I cannot work without a foot or a hand."

"Not so great a penalty as that, farmer. The tip of one finger or toe." She extended her own hand. "You may choose which one to sacrifice in obedience to the Arxon." The man was close to fainting. Reaching through depression for some kindness, she told him, "The tip of the smallest finger on the left hand will leave you at only a small disadvantage. Here, put it out to me." The beancounter took his shaking, roughened hand by the nail-bitten phalange, and held it tightly over the ceramic sluice bowl. She murmured a cantrip, and the machines of the Arxon hummed through her own fingers. The room filled with the sickening stench of rotted meat and she was holding a pitted white bone, her fingers slimy. The farmer lurched away from the desk, shoving the rancid tip of his finger into his mouth like a burned child, flung it away again at the taste. His face was pale. In a moment his rage might outmatch his fear. Bonida wiped her fingers, rose, handed him a document attesting to his payment. "See the nurse on your way out, Mr. Bai. She will bandage your wound." She laid her hand upon him once again, felt the virtue tremble. "It should bud and regrow itself within a year, or sooner. Here is a word of advice: next season, do not tarry in meeting your obligations. Good sday."

She poured water into the bowl, washed and dried, then in a muttered flash of steam flushed away the stink of decomposition together with the scum in the bowl. The beancounter sighed, found another bill of particulars, announced the next name. "Ernő Szabó. Office Four."

§

Marmalade the cat was waiting on her doorstep. He averted his nose.

"Madame, you smell disgusting."

"I beg your pardon!" Bonida was affronted. From childhood, she had been raised to a strict regimen of hygiene, as befitted a future maiden of the Sodality. Poor as she was, by comparison with the finest in the Regio, nonetheless she insisted on bathing once a sweek at the springs, and was strict with her teeth brushing. Although, admittedly, that onion-flavored brioche at lunch—

"The smell of death clings to you."

The beancounter squeezed her jaw tight, flung off her bonnet, hitched her provender bag higher on her shoulder. Without thinking, she hid her right hand inside a fold of her robe. Catching herself, she deliberately withdrew it and waved her inky fingers in front of the beast.

"It is my skill, my duty, my profession," she told him in a thin voice. "If you have objections to my trade, I will not trouble you to share my small repast." But when she made to open her door, the animal was through it before her, sinuous and sly, for a moment more the quicksilver courtier than the bully.

"Enough of your nonsense," the cat said, settling on a rug. "Milk, and be quick about it."

The audacity was breathtaking, and indeed the breath caught for an instant in her throat, then choked out in a guffaw. Shaking her head, Bonida took the stoppered jug from her bag and poured them both a draught. In a vase on the table, nightblooms had sagged, their green leaves parched and drooping.

"What do you want, m'sieur? Clearly you are not stalking me because you treasure my fragrance." The beancounter emptied the stale water, refilled the vase, touched the posy. Virtue flowed. It was not hers; she was merely the conduit, or so her mother had instructed her. The flowers revived in an ordinary miracle of renewal; heavy scents filled the room, perhaps masking her own alleged odor. Why did she care? An animal, after all, even if one gifted with speech and effrontery.

The cat lapped up the milk in silence, licked his whiskers clean, then sat back neatly, nostrils twitching at the scent. "Your mother Elisetta."

"She died three years ago, during a ruction in the square." It still wrenched at her heart to speak of it. "So you knew her," she said, suddenly certain of it. And yet her late mother had never mentioned so singular an acquaintance. Another mystery of the

Sodality, no doubt. Like the marmalade cat himself.

"I introduced her to your father."

"I have no father."

The cat gave one sharp sardonic cough, as if trying to relieve himself of a hairball. "So you burst forth full-formed from your mother's forehead?"

"What?"

"Never mind. Nobody ever remembers the old stories. Especially the coded ones."

"What?"

"Your lap."

"You wouldn't prefer that I go out and bathe first?"

"Actually yes, but we don't have time. Come on, woman, make a lap."

She did so, and the beast leapt with supernatural lightness, circled once to make a nest, and snuggled down. His head, she realized, was almost as large as her own. He slitted his eyes and emitted an unbearably comforting noise. A sort of deep, drumming, rhythmic music. Her mouth opened in surprise. She had read of this in old verses of romance. Marmalade was purring.

"Your father was the Arxon," the cat told her, then. "Still is, in fact."

§

At Ostler's Corner, on the advice of the cat, the beancounter engaged the services of a pedlar. Marmalade sprang into the rickshaw cabin, waited with ill-disguised irritation as a groom handed Bonida up with her luncheon basket and settled her comfortably, accepting a coin after a murmured consultation with his bank. The great brute stirred at a kick, its reptilian hide fifteen shades of green, and lurched its feet into their cage quill constraints, tail flared beneath the platform. Soon its immense quadriceps and hams were pumping furiously, pedaling their rickshaw with increasing celerity along the central thoroughfare of the Regio and out into the countryside, making for the towering cliffs that formed the near-vertical foothills of the Skyfallen Heights. Now and then it registered its grievance at this usage, trying to wrench its snout far enough to bite at its tormentors, but sturdy draught-poles held its head forward.

"We approach the equatorial ridge of Iapetus," the cat told her. "Does your Sodality teach you this much? That this small world has its breathable air held close and warmed by design and contrivance? That its very gravity is augmented by deformations?"

"Certain matters I may not speak of," she said, averting her gaze, "as you must know since you profess knowledge of my mother and her guild." Eye-yapper-tus, she thought. Whatever could that—

"Yes, yes," Marmalade said. "Elisetta learned the best part of her arcane doctrines from me, so you can rest easy on that score."

"Ha! So you might assert if you intended to hornswoggle me."

The cat uttered a wheezing laugh. "Hornswoggle? Ha! You are not my type, madame."

Bonida tightened her lips. "You are offensive, m'sieur." She was silent long enough to convey her displeasure, but then said, "I see we are drawing to a stop. Will you tell me finally why you have lured me out to this inhospitable territory?"

"Why, I have information to impart to the daughter of the Arxon." He leapt lightly from the cabin, waited as she lowered herself, hampered by her hamper. "Stay here," he snarled at the pedlar. "We shall return within the hour."

"Why must I take orders from a beast?" the reptile asked, slaver at his lips. "I am indentured to humans, not cats."

"Hold your tongue, you, or you'll be catmeat by dawn."

Something in Marmalade's tone gave the great green creature pause; it fell silent and averted its gaze, withdrawing its long toes from the quills and settling uncomfortably between the traces. "I shall be here, your highness," it said in a bitter tone.

"Follow me, woman," said the cat. "You can leave your picnic basket. Wait, bring the milk jug."

"You can't seriously expect me to climb this cliff?"

"There are more ways than one to skin a—" Marmalade broke off with a cough. "You are familiar with the principle of the tunnel?" They stood before a concealed cleft in the rock face. He went forward in a graceful leap and vanished into the shadows.

§

It was like finding oneself immured inside an enormous pipe, perhaps a garden hose for watering the stars, Bonida decided. The walls were smooth as ice, but warm to the touch. Something thrummed, deeper than the ear could hear, audible through skin and bone. She stood at the edge of a passage from infinity (or so it seemed in the faint light) at her left to infinity at her right.

"This is where Father Time built his AI composites," the cat said, and his voice, thinned, seemed to vanish into the huge long, wide space. "It's an accelerator as big as a world. Here is where the Skydark dyson swarms were congealed from the emptiness and flung into the sky."

"The what? Were what?"

"The Embee," said the cat absently. He was looking for something. His paw touched a place in the smooth wall, raised from it an elaborately figured cartouche, smote it thrice. They rose into the middle of the air and rushed forward down the infinite corridor, the wind of their motion somehow almost wholly held in abeyance. If it were not for that breeze, they might have been suspended motionless. Yet somehow, through her terror, she sensed tremendous velocity. "Don't drop the milk." He added, at her scowl, "Embee—the MBrain. The M-Brane. Not to be confused with the Mem-brain."

"I have no idea what you're talking about."

"Oh, never mind."

She puzzled it out, as they fled into an endlessness of the

same. "You're saying that the Skyfallen Heights did not fall? That it was built?"

"Oh, it was built, all right, and it fell from the sky. Father Time broke up another moon and rained it down like silt in a strip around the equator. Compiled the accelerator, you might say." The cat, afloat in the air, gave her a feline grin. "Two thirds of it has worn away by now. It was a long time ago. But it can still get you from here to there in a hurry."

The breeze was gone. They had stopped, or paused. The cat lifted his head. A vast rumbling above them; something was opening. They rose, flung upward like bubbles in a flute, and then moved fast in the great darkness, yet still breathing without effort, warm enough, the curving contusion of the Skydark to one side—the Embee, the cat had named it, if that is what he had meant—the smaller ring-cradled sphere on the other, and, directly above, something like a dull ruby the size of a palace falling to crush them, or rather they fell upward into it. And were inside its embrace, light blossoming to dazzle her eyes, so that she cried out and did in fact drop the jug, which shattered on a surface like rippled marble, spilling milk in a spray that caught the cat's left ear and whiskers. He turned in fury, raised one clawed paw, made to strike, held his blow at the last instant from scratching a welt in her flesh.

"Clumsy! Oh well." He visibly forced himself to sink down on all four limbs, slitting his eyes, then rose again. "Come and meet your parents, you lump."

§

Her mother was dead and ceremonially returned to Cycling. Bonida knew this with bitter regret, for she had stood by the open casket and pressed the cold pale hand, speaking aloud in her grief, hopelessly, the cantrip of renewal. Was there a trembling of the virtue? She could not be sure. Imagination, then. Nothing, nothing. They swiftly closed the casket and whisked it away. But no, here she was after all, at first solemn and then breaking into a smile to see her daughter running in tears to catch up her hands and kiss them, Bonida on her knees, shaking her head in disbelief, eyes swimming.

"Mother Elisetta!"

"Darling girl! And Meister Marmalade." She curtsied to the cat.

"Hi, toots."

"Now allow me to introduce you to your sire."

A presence made itself known to them.

"Welcome, my daughter. I am Ouranos. We have a task for you to fulfill, child. For the Sodality. For the world."

The beancounter recoiled, releasing her mother's hands. She stared wildly about her.

"This is a machine," she cried in revulsion.

From the corner of her eye she seemed to see a form like a man.

The cat said, "Enough sniffling and jumping at shadows. We have work to do."

"How can I be the daughter of a machine?" Bonita remained on her knees, closed in upon herself, whimpering. "This is deceit! All of it! My mother is dead, this isn't her. Take me away, you wretched animal. Return me home and then stay the hell away from me."

"No deception in this, my darling." Her mother touched the crown of her head in a gesture Bonida had known from infancy, bringing fresh tears. "You are upset, and we understand why. It was cruel to allow you to think I had been taken into death, but a necessary cruelty. We had the most pressing and urgent reasons, dear child. We had tasks to perform which brooked no interference. The night has a thousand thousand eyes. Now it is your turn to embrace your destiny. Come, stand up beside me, the hour grows late."

The presence she could not quite see, no matter how swiftly she turned her eyes, said in its deep beautiful voice, "The light of the bright world dies with the dying Sun."

"What is the 'Sun'?" asked the beancounter.

§

Elisetta, High Governor of the Sodality of Righteous Knowledge, formerly dead, now brow-furrowed and certainly alive, gestured fore and aft. "Open."

Bow and stern of the ruby clarified and were gone: blackness ahead, spattered at random with pinpricks of sharp light, save for the ringed globe that was now as broad as a hand near one's face, faintly luminous; the great contusion behind, glowing faintly with a dim crimson so deep it tricked the eye to suppose it was darkness, a large round spot upon its countenance that dwindled as she watched. The spot was, she realized with a jolt, her world entire. In the starlight, it seemed that one half of the spot was faintly lighter than the other.

"That great dimness conceals the Sun," her mother said, with a sweeping motion of her arm. "Hidden within the hundred veils of genius we call the Skydark. You have heard this story a dozen times from my own lips, Bonida, since you were a child at my breast, veiled like the Sun in allegory."

Silent, astonished, rueful, the beancounter regarded immensity, the dwindling piebald spot. "That is our world, falling away behind us," she ventured.

"Iapetus, yes," the cat said. "A world like a walnut, with a raised welt at its waist."

"And what is a wal—" There was no point. This terminology, she divined, was not meant to tease nor torment her; it was a lexicon written to account for a universe larger than her own. She'd heard this term "Iapetus" before, from the cat's mouth. So the world had a name, like a woman or a cat; not just the World. "All right, enough of that. Where are we going? To that other... world, ahead?" It pleased her, stiffened her spine, that she had said Where are we going and not Where are you taking me.

"To Father Time, yes, for an audience. Saturn, as your ancient forebears called him. Father of us all, in some ways." That was the unseeable presence speaking. She nearly wrenched her neck trying to trap him, but he was off again in some moving blind place, evading her. A machine, she told herself. Rebuked herself, rather. Not a man. How could a thing like that claim affinity, let alone paternity? Yet was there not affinity between humans and machines, in the utterance of a cantrip, the invocation of power? If water boiled and steamed in her bucket, that was no doing of hers. She had acknowledged that, and yet daily forgot the fact, since she was a child, learning the runes and sigils and codes of action. When she rotted the flesh from some hapless infractor, or brought some dead thing back to life and growth, that was again the machines, operating her like a machine, perhaps, making her own flesh their tool. It was a horrifying reflection. Little wonder, she told herself, that we turn our faces from its recognition.

"Why?" A touch of iciness entered her tone. "And why have you and this appalling animal abducted me?"

The cat regarded her with equal coldness, turned and stalked off to the farthest end of the craft, which was not far, and gazed studiously back at the Skydark. Her mother said, "Bonida, you are unkind. But no doubt you have a right to your...impatience."

"My anger, if you must know, mother." The tingling was returned to her fingers, and she knew, horrified, that if she were to seize Elisetta's arm in this mood the flesh would blacken and fall from the woman's bones. As, perhaps, who knew, it had been recovered in reverse following her death; she had seen her mother's dead body, attempted to revive her, perhaps *had* revived her. None of this was tolerable. She would not go mad. Quivering, she held her arms down at her sides. "You consort with machines and gods and talking cats. You parcel out to me fragments of lost knowledge—or plain fabrications, for all I know. We fall between worlds, and you refuse to, to...." She broke off, face pale.

Softly, the older woman said, "We refuse nothing, daughter. Be still for a moment. Seek calmness. In a few moments, you will know everything, and then you will help us make a choice."

"Fat lot of use she'll be," said the cat in a surly voice, without turning his head. "We could have had milk, but she smashed the jug. Unreliable, I say. If you ask me—"

"Quiet!" The unseen figure had an edge to his tone, commanding, and Marmalade cocked his whiskers but fell silent. "Child," Ouranos told her, "something very important is about to happen. Everything held dear by human people and machines and animals is at stake. Not just our survival, but the persistence of the world itself, of history stretching a billion years and more into the mysteries of our creation."

The beancounter was feeling very tired. She looked around for a chair or a cushion, and found one right behind her, comfortable and handsomely brocaded. She felt sure it had not been there a moment earlier. Tightening her teeth against each other, she let herself slump into the chair. Her mother also was seating herself, and the cat walked by from the stern with an attitude of hauteur and lofted into Elisetta's lap, where he immediately began his droning purr, ignoring Bonida. The unseeable presence remained just out of sight. Wonderful! Would it not have been more melodramatic for a third chair to manifest, so she might witness its cushions sag under invisible buttocks?

Something took the ruby into its grasp and they were held motionless above the great rings, an expanse of faint ice and ruptured stones, some as large as their craft, mostly pebbles or sand or dust, like a winter roadway in the sky yet swirling ever so slowly. Far away, but closer than ever before, the bruised globe showed stripes of various dim hues, and a swirl that might have been a vast storm seen from above.

"Call us Saturn," a powerful, resonant voice said within the cabin. It was unseen, and a presence, but not her father the machine. And the beancounter knew that it was also a machine, yet beyond doubt a person, too, of such depth and majesty that its own unseen presence rendered them unutterably insignificant. Somehow, though, this realization did not crush her spirit. She glanced at her mother. Elisetta was watching her, calm, wise, accepting, encouraging. How I do love her, Bonida thought, even though she treated me so cruelly by pretending death. But perhaps it was no fault of her mother's. Sometimes one has no choice. Her own employment, for one.

"We offer you a choice," the voice of the world Saturn told them all. Marmalade was now seated on the carpet, upright on his haunches, seemingly respectful. What was the animal plotting this time? "But it must be an informed choice. Permit me to join you."

An immense tawny beast crouched in their midst, larger than a human, with a golden mane that rose behind its formidable head. When it spoke again, its rumbling voice was a roar held in check.

"Call me Aslan, if you wish."

Marmalade had leapt backward, teeth and claws bared, his own fur bristling. Now he sat down again, slightly askew, and turned his face away. "Oh, give me a break."

The great creature shot him a quizzical look, shrugged those powerful cat-like shoulders. "As you please. Look here—"

§

A hundred voices in muted conversation, like a gathering for supper before the Sodality Plenary, then louder, a thousand chattering, a million million, a greater number, all speaking at once, voices weaving a pattern as large and multifarious as the accreted skyfallen materials of the great ridge circling her world, so that she must clap her hands to her ears, but she had no hands and must scream in the lemon-yellow glare of an impossibly brilliant light that—

"Too bright!" she did scream, then.

The light shed its painful intensity, subsided step by step to a point of roseate glow, and the voices muffled their chorus. She gazed down past the sparkling icy rings to the globe of Saturn, down through its storms and sleet of helium and hydrogen to the shell of metallic hydrogen wrapping its iron core. A seed fell. A long explosion crackled across the lifeless frigid surface world, drawing heat and power from the energies of Saturn's core, snapping one of the molecules after another into ingenious patterns braided and interpenetrating, flowing charges, magnetic fluxes. The voices were the song of those circuits, those—memristors, she knew, somehow. Not to be confused with the Mem-brain, the damnable cat had joked, and now Bonida smiled, getting the modest joke. Skeins of molecules linked like the inner parts of a brain, sparks of information, calculation, awareness, conscious-ness—

Oyarsa, you might say, the great feline manifest told her. She knew instantly what he meant: he was the ruling entity of this planet, the mind of which the planet was the brain and body. Not quite right, though: not he but they. A community of minds linked by light and entanglement (and yes, now she understood that as well, and, well, everything, at least in its numberless parts).

"How did you make the Skyfallen Heights, and why?"

Aslan told her, "The smallest of small questions. The cat has already told you. How do you make a trumpet? Take a hole and wrap tin around it."

"Gustav Mahler," Marmalade said, whiskers flicking. "You could say the same about his symphonies. Bah! Trumpets? Give me blues, man."

Symphonies, trumpets, the composer Mahler, a thousand riches from lost Earth: it flooded her mind without overflowing.

"Yes, I know that much, but why? To build the Skydark, yes, but why?" It was an immense construction, she saw, the Field of Arbol uttered from imagination into reality, sphere within sphere of memristors, sucking every erg of energy from the hidden Sun at its core, a community of godlike beings that surpassed their builder as the Father of Time surpassed, perhaps, whatever ancient beings had brought him/them into existence. But why? But why?

"All the children ask that question," said her mother, smiling. "Why, Bonida, for *joy*, as the Sodality has always taught. For endless renewal. For the recovery of the world. Taking a hole and wrapping everything important around it."

"More arrant sentimentality," said the cat, looking disgusted.

"You are a most offensive creature," the beancounter said reprovingly, although she tended to agree with him. "Here, come sit upon my lap." The animal shot her a surprised look, then did as she suggested, springing, circling, snuggling down, heavy orange head leaned back against her modest breast. She let one hand stroke down his coat, and again. "So what is this question we are meant to address?"

The lion rose, looked from one human to the other, and his glance took in as well the rumbling cat and the unseen presence.

"We are considering terminating our life."

Elisetta pressed forward, shocked, all tranquility dispelled. Her voice cracked: "You must not! What would become of us?"

"That is not the question we wish to put to you, although it has a bearing. Yours is not the species that created us, before they departed, to whom we are beholden, yet you are living beings like those creators. We in turn created the great Minds that cloak the Sun, and built their habitation. Now they, too, are at the end of their dealings with this universe. They know all that might be known, and have imagined all that might be done within the greater landscape of universes. So now they propose to voyage into deepest time, to the ends of eternity. Perhaps something greater awaits them there."

Bonita's own small mind, acknowledging its smallness, reeled at the images flooding to her from the demigod whose own life and purpose were complete at last. Stars and galaxies of stars would fling themselves apart into the night, driven by the power of that darkness, their flaring illumination fading, finally, flickering, dying. All the multiple manifestations of cosmos torn apart and lost in a dying whisper. Her mood summoned from the treasure house the Adagietto from that composer Mahler's Fifth Symphony, and she sank into its tinted, tearful melancholy. Yet in the frigid blackness and emptiness she detected... something. A lure, a promise, at the very least a teasing hint of laughter. How could the Skydark not follow that trace to eternity? How could she?

"Off," she told the cat, and Marmalade sprang away, less

offended than one might have expected. She stood up and took her mother's hand. "We are the deputies of your makers, then? You and the Skydark require our...what? Permission? Leave to die, or to depart?"

"Yes."

"And what's to become of us?"

"You will remain for as long as we burn." A vision was placed before them of the ringed world falling in upon itself, crushed into terrifying density, alight with the energies of compression. And Iapetus circling that new Sun, this visible star, unshielded, unveiled, but barren of mind. The agony of loss slashed tears from her eyes. Yet it was Saturn's decision.

"Can we go instead with the Skydark? The Embee? May we share that voyage?"

"Thought you'd never ask," said Marmalade. "And you, Madame High Governor, and Ouranos, Lord Arxon, do you concur with the wisdom and daring of this young woman?"

"I—" Her mother hesitated, gone once into death and retrieved by the gift of her child, looking from Bonita to the machine in which they stood. "Yes, yes of course. And you, sir?"

"We shall attend you, Lord Marmalade," said the unseen presence. "Even unto the ends of eternity. It will be an awfully big adventure."

A qualm brought the beancounter an abrupt pang. "What of the pedlar we hired? He's still waiting for us, poor creature. He might not be so happy at the prospect. Who are we to make such a choice for a whole world?"

"He'll get over it," said the cat. "And hey, if not you, who?"

§

The sky rolled up, and they set sail into forever.

ALL SUMMER LONG

Mother was really pleased when Dad brought the new robot home. Our housekeeper had just graduated as an accountant after nine years of night school and left us, to start work with H&R Block up the road.

Dad honked his car horn out the front when he got home this day. He honked it again, impatiently, when nobody came out. After the third noisy honk I peeked out the window to see what the fuss was about and saw him sitting in the car, at the curb, with the window down. I passed this news on to Mother, who told me, "Go and see what your father wants, Davy, I've got this awful stuff all over my hands."

It was true. She was trying to make dinner for us, using something called a recipe. The kitchen was covered in a fine layer of white flour, and there were two broken eggs on the floor. The cat was licking up the yolks and getting under foot. Something was smoking in the microwave. I turned it off before the smoke alarm was triggered and the fire brigade came rushing around.

"Yabba, Dad," I yelled, wandering down the path.

Dad yelled back from the car window, "Where's your mother, Davy?" He had that look you get when you're bursting with exciting news and nobody is paying any attention. "Tell her to come out, I've got a treat for her."

"Cool." I wandered back to the kitchen. Mother was trying to shoo Perdida the cat away from the smashed eggs. I didn't know cats ate raw eggs, but then our cat is fat and greedy and would snatch the burger off your lap if you let her. "Dad's got a surprise for you, Mother."

"I've got one for him, too," Mother said crankily. "No dinner."

"Oh boy," called Marj from the study room, "take-out! Can we have Mongolian?"

By the time we'd all trooped out the front door and down the path, Dad was locking the car. Something short and wide and dark green was propped on the grass strip next to him. It looked as if a new shrub had sprung up over-night. Well, faster than that, because it hadn't been there a minute earlier.

Dad walked toward us up the path with a pleased grin, and the shrub followed. Mother gave a squeal.

"Darling! A household robot! You said we couldn't afford one!"

"Bratachari in Engineering has arranged for some of us to have one on extended loan," Dad said, giving Mother a big smooch, and beaming at us kids. "Beta test. The Moravec company has made about a thousand robots available. We can evaluate its performance."

"What's it called?" Marj asked, staring down at the moving shrub. "Why does it look like a big plant if it's a robot? I thought they were silvery or covered in plastic or something?"

"It's a Moravec bush robot," Dad told us. "See, its arms look like branches and they have smaller arms at the ends that look like twigs, and they have really fine manipulators at the end like prickles."

"Herb," I said. "That's his name."

"How do you know? That's a stupid name for a robot."

"No it's not," I said, and pulled her hair. She yelped, and Dad gave me a clip over the ear. "It's 'Herb' because he looks like something that grows in the garden, get it?"

"How do you know it's a 'him'," Marj said smugly. "Maybe it's a 'she'. I reckon she's called Rose."

"Whatever," Dad said. "Davy got in first, so Herb it is."

Marj gave me a sour look and went inside. Mrs. McGunzel, across the road, was standing at her open front door, gazing at our new robot. Mother waved to her, and after a moment she waved back, but she looked a bit scared. I don't know why, I thought Herbie was supercool.

"Does it talk?"

"Yes, up to a point, but we need to introduce ourselves first." By this stage we were assembled in the living room, gathered in a half-circle around the robot. Dad pulled the instruction manual out of his briefcase and flipped through the first few pages. "We were told how to do this at the office, but I don't quite recall how to— Ah, here we are. Robot 47D95, instruction mode on."

"Good evening, sir or madam."

I gave a hoot of laughter, and Dad flushed. He was always sensitive about his slightly high-pitched voice, but I reckon the robot was just pulling his leg.

"That's 'sir'," he said crossly. "Your name is 'Herb' or 'Herbie,' okay? And I'm Roland FitzSimmons, your new owner." He went through the rest of the introductions.

"Glad to you meet you," Herb told us. "I would like to begin my duties now. May I prepare dinner for the family?"

"Oh, bless you," Mother blurted. "Do you cook?"

"I am programmed for fifty-two national cuisines," the robot told her. "Afghani, American, Australian, Balinese, Caribbean, Chinese, Creole, Deli, Egyptian, Ethiopian—"

"Do you do pizza?" I asked it.

There was a moment's silence. "Certainly, Davy." I thought it sounded a bit offended. "Can someone direct me to the kitchen?"

The robot moved in a mysterious way, sort of gliding on its branches and twigs. Perdida the cat freaked when it slid into the kitchen, and leaped on to the nearest bench, all her fur sticking out and her back arched.

"This place is disgusting," Herb said. "I shall have to clean up first. Please remove the domestic animal."

Mother was insulted, but you could see the robot's point. She just wasn't very good at this food preparation caper. Marj went and retrieved Perdida, smoothed down her ruffled fur, and took her and Mother into the living room. I stayed in the kitchen door, watching Herb. He kind of flattened out into a turtle, or what a turtle would look like if it had been stepped on by an elephant. More like a surfboard.

It slid easily over the kitchen floor, and after it was done there was no sign of spilled flour or broken egg shells, and the bits of orange peel I'd dropped in the corner when I missed the trashbin were gone. Herb had...well, he'd sort of eaten everything, I suppose. He extended upward once more and became a bush, then kept extending and became a kind of short tree. His branches swept out across the kitchen benches, sucking up the mess and straightening everything out. It was a miracle of applied science.

Then Herb found the larder and refrigerator and the stove and the microwave and started on dinner. Awesome! That robot spun around the kitchen like a green whirlwind, opening jars, laying out pans, mixing and blending and pouring and tidying up as it went. Dad and I stared at each other in amazement. Mother came back and looked suspiciously at Herb's work, and then nodded. She was won over, I could tell. Perdida sulked in the corner of the living room, and slunk under the couch when Herb brought out piping hot pizzas to the dining table.

"Can it do homework?" Marj asked, wiping a thick gloopy strand of cheese off her mouth.

"You'll do your homework yourself, young lady," Mother told her. "But it can help you tidy your room. That will give you plenty of spare time for your studies."

"Can he sleep in my room?" I asked.

"The robot will stay downstairs," Dad said. "It can go into its dormant phase in the closet, since we won't need brooms and the vacuum cleaner any more. Well, until the trial ends, anyway."

"I shall sleep on the roof, thank you," Herb said. "I collect power from the sun's rays, like a flower or a tree. I am an ecologically friendly mechanism."

When we got up next morning, the house smelled wonderfully of hot toast and even hotter coffee. Herb had made breakfast for us all. Even Perdida was purring—Herb had poured her a bowl of milk, and put out some Kat Crunchies in her bowl, after cleaning it. I couldn't wait to tell the other kids at school about our keen robot.

That afternoon, I rode back quickly on my trail bike in the hot summer sun so I could see what Herb was up to. I brought Ken and Michio so they could meet Herb. When we banging in through the front door, Mother was out at her bridge game and I couldn't find Herb anywhere. We grabbed some cookies and beverages and went out the back. Herb was soaking up the rays next to the pool.

"Hey! It's all flat! You said it was like a tree."

"It can change shape," I told Michio. "I wonder if he can float?"

"Let's toss him in the pool," Ken suggested.

"Well, I don't know—"

The others ran across and grabbed the flat robot and lifted him off the grass. Herb looked like a green flying saucer. He must have been pretty heavy, because they had a bit of trouble moving him. They shoved him toward the edge of the pool, and he slid in to the blue water and sank.

"Uh-oh."

"You idiots!" I shouted. "Do you know how much one of those robots costs?"

A dark green snorkel rose above the surface of the pool and quested about. Herb must have been able to see through it, because it pointed in our direction.

"This is very pleasant," Herb told us through the snorkel. "Thank you."

"Our pleasure, dude," Ken said with a smirk. "Hey, maybe this robot's a surfer!"

Herb floated up to the top of the pool. His body was flatter than ever, like a plate. He moved back and forth slowly, the edges of his body kind of paddling with a thousand tiny tendrils.

"Hey, yeah, he'd make a great board. Come on, let's show him some surfing videos and see if he can morph into, like, the world's best interactive board."

Herb slid up the side of the pool and turned back into a shrub. The water just kind of fell off him. Skin like a dolphin, amazing. We took him inside and sat him down in front of the TV set and showed him some of Dad's old surfer movies. Herb really loved *Crystal Rider*, you could tell.

That night we ate Lebanese, because Mother insisted on it. I wasn't too sure at first, but Herb whipped up such a great spread with mouth-watering smells and tastes that I wolfed down everything on my plate and asked for more. Herbie cleaned up quietly while we watched some television, and then put himself away neatly in the closet. He must have charged up enough in the sun by the pool.

Next morning he was gone. No delightful morning smells of ham and eggs and toast. Not even a note. Dad was frantic. He phoned a couple of friends from work who also had robots out on beta test. All the robots were gone.

News reports started coming in from traffic helicopters. Strange green bushes were on the march. People were panicking. Cars ran into the curb. Dogs fled in fear. Little old ladies were being helped across the street by shrubs. The streets the shrubs passed along had never been cleaner. Inside an hour, it was obvious all the robots were heading for the ocean.

And that's where Herbie is now. I don't know which one he is, but I can see them on the TV news—hundreds of glistening green surfboards, without riders, out there under the summer sun riding the waves. It looks weird, I have to say, all those boards with no surfers hanging five on them and paddling out to catch a great wave. The boards do it all by themselves, skimming out into the deep blue like dolphins, turning, waiting for the wave, moving faster, catching it, hovering for a heart-stopping moment at the very lip of the breaking surf and then riding that sucker in, tens and hundreds of green surfboards flying in the sun, singing together and synthesizing their own guitar and drum backing, singing old Beach Boys hits from last century. It made my hair stand on end. I have to tell you, it made me wish I was a robot surfer.

UNDER THE
MOONS OF VENUS

1.

In the long, hot, humid afternoon, Blackett obsessively paced off the outer dimensions of the Great Temple of Petra against the black asphalt of the deserted car parks, trying to recapture the pathway back to Venus. Faint rectangular lines still marked the empty spaces allocated to staff vehicles long gone from the campus, stretching on every side like the equations in some occult geometry of invocation. Later, as shadows stretched across the all-but-abandoned industrial park, he considered again the possibility that he was trapped in delusion, even psychosis. At the edge of an overgrown patch of dried lawn, he found a crushed Pepsi can, a bent yellow plastic straw protruding from it. He kicked it idly.

"Thus I refute Berkeley," he muttered, with a half smile. The can twisted, fell back on the grass; he saw that a runner of bind weed wrapped its flattened waist.

He walked back to the sprawling house he had appropriated, formerly the residence of a wealthy CEO. Glancing at his IWC Flieger Chrono aviator's watch, he noted that he should arrive there ten minutes before his daily appointment with the therapist.

2.

Cool in a chillingly expensive pale blue Mila Schön summer frock, her carmine toenails brightly painted in her open Ferragamo Penelope sandals, Clare regarded him: lovely, sly, professionally compassionate. She sat across from him on the front porch of the old house, rocking gently in the suspended glider.

"Your problem," the psychiatrist told him, "is known in our trade as lack of affect. You have shut down and locked off your emotional responses. You should know, Robert, that this isn't healthy or sustainable."

"Of course I know that," he said, faintly irritated by her condescension. "Why else would I be consulting you? Not," he said pointedly, "that it is doing me much good."

"It takes time, Robert. As you know."

3.

Later, when Clare was gone, Blackett sat beside his silent sound system and poured two fingers of Hennessy XO brandy. It was the best he had been able to find in the largely depleted supermarket, or at any rate the least untenable for drinking purposes. He took the spirits into his mouth and felt fire run down his throat. Months earlier, he had found a single bottle of Mendis Coconut brandy in the cellar of an enormous country house. Gone now. He sat a little longer, rose, cleaned his teeth and made his toilet, drank a full glass of faintly brackish water from the tap. He found a Philip Glass CD and placed it in the mouth of the player, then went to bed. Glass's repetitions and minimal novelty eased him into sleep. He woke at 3 in the morning, heart thundering. Silence absolute. Blackett cursed himself for forgetting to press the automatic repeat key on the CD player. Glass had fallen silent, along with most of the rest of the human race. He touched his forehead. Sweat coated his fingers.

4.

In the morning, he drove in a stolen car to the industrial park's air field, rolled the Cesna 182 out from the protection of its hangar, and refueled its tanks. Against the odds, the electrically powered pump and other systems remained active, drawing current from the black arrays of solar cells oriented to the south and east, swiveling during the daylight hours to follow the apparent track of the sun. He made his abstracted, expert run through the checklist, flicked on the radio by reflex. A hum of carrier signal, nothing more. The control tower was deserted. Blackett ran the Cessna onto the slightly cracked asphalt and took off into a brisk breeze. He flew across fields going to seed, visible through sparklingly clear air. Almost no traffic moved on the roads below him. Two or three vehicles threw up a haze of dust from the untended roadway, and one laden truck crossed his path, apparently cluttered to overflowing with furniture and bedding. It seemed the ultimate in pointlessness—why not appropriate a suitable house, as he had done, and make do with its appointments? Birds flew up occasionally in swooping flocks, careful to avoid his path.

Before noon, he was landing on the coast at the deserted Matagorda Island air force base a few hundred yards from the ocean. He sat for a moment, hearing his cooling engines ticking, and gazed at the two deteriorating Stearman biplanes that rested in the salty open air. They were at least a century old, at one time lovingly restored for air shows and aerobatic displays. Now their fabric sagged, striped red and green paint peeling from their fuselages and wings. They sagged into the hot tarmac, rubber tires rotted by the corrosive oceanfront air and the sun's pitiless ultraviolet.

Blackett left his own plane in the open. He did not intend to remain here long. He strolled to the end of the runway and into the long grass stretching to the ocean. Socks and trouser legs were covered quickly in clinging burrs. He reached the sandy shore as the sun stood directly overhead. After he had walked for half a mile along the strand, wishing he had thought to bring a hat, a dog crossed the sand and paced alongside, keeping its distance.

"You're Blackett," the dog said.

"Speaking."

"Figured it must have been you. Rare enough now to run into a human out here."

Blackett said nothing. He glanced at the dog, feeling no enthusiasm for a conversation. The animal was healthy enough, and well fed, a red setter with long hair that fluffed up in the tangy air. His paws left a trail across the white sand, paralleling the tracks Blackett had made. Was there some occult meaning in this simplest of geometries? If so, it would be erased soon enough, as the ocean moved in, impelled by the solar tide, and lazily licked the beach clean.

Seaweed stretched along the edge of the sluggish water, dark green, stinking. Out of breath, he sat and looked disconsolately across the slow, flat waves of the diminished tide. The dog trotted by, threw itself down in the sand a dozen feet away. Blackett knew he no longer dared sit here after nightfall, in a dark alive with thousands of brilliant pinpoint stars, a planet or two, and no Moon. Never again a Moon. Once he had ventured out here after the sun went down, and low in the deep indigo edging the horizon had seen the clear distinct blue disk of the evening star, and her two attendant satellites, one on each side of the planet. Ganymede, with its thin atmosphere still intact, remained palest brown. Luna, at that distance, was a bright pinpoint orb, her pockmarked face never again to be visible to the naked eye of an Earthly viewer beneath her new, immensely deep carbon dioxide atmosphere.

He noticed that the dog was creeping cautiously toward him, tail wagging, eyes averted except for the occasional swift glance.

"Look," he said, "I'd rather be alone."

The dog sat up and uttered a barking laugh. It swung its

head from side to side, conspicuously observing the hot, empty strand.

"Well, bub, I'd say you've got your wish, in spades."

"Nobody has swum here in years, apart from me. This is an old air force base, it's been decommissioned for...."

He trailed off. It was no answer to the point the animal was making. Usually at this time of year, Blackett acknowledged to himself, other beaches, more accessible to the crowds, would be swarming with shouting or whining children, mothers waddling or slumped, baking in the sun under SP 50 lotions, fat men eating snacks from busy concession stands, vigorous swimmers bobbing in white-capped waves. Now the empty waves crept in, onto the tourist beaches as they did here, like the flattened, poisoned combers at the site of the Exxon Valdez oil spill, twenty years after men had first set foot on the now absent Moon.

"It wasn't my idea," he said. But the dog was right; this isolation was more congenial to him than otherwise. Yet the yearning to rejoin the rest of the human race on Venus burned in his chest like angina.

"Not like I'm blaming you, bub." The dog tilted its handsome head. "Hey, should have said, I'm Sporky."

Blackett inclined his own head in reply. After a time, Sporky said, "You think it's a singularity excursion, right?"

He got to his feet, brushed sand from his legs and trousers. "I certainly don't suspect the hand of Jesus. I don't think I've been Left Behind."

"Hey, don't go away now." The dog jumped up, followed him at a safe distance. "It could be aliens, you know."

"You talk too much," Blackett said.

5.

As he landed, later in the day, still feeling refreshed from his hour in the water, he saw through the heat curtains of rising air a rather dirty precinct vehicle drive through the unguarded gate and onto the runway near the hangars. He taxied in slowly, braked, opened the door. The sergeant climbed out of his Ford Crown Victoria, cap off, waving it to cool his florid face.

"Saw you coming in, Doc," Jacobs called. "Figured you might like a lift back. Been damned hot out today, not the best walking weather."

There was little point in arguing. Blackett clamped the red tow bar to the nose wheel, steered the Cessna backward into the hangar, heaved the metal doors closed with an echoing rumble. He climbed into the cold interior of the Ford. Jacobs had the air-conditioning running at full bore, and a noxious country and western singer wailing from the sound system. Seeing his guest's frown, the police officer grinned broadly and turned the hideous noise down.

"You have a visitor waiting," he said. His grin verged on the lewd. Jacobs drove by the house twice a day, part of his self-imposed duty, checking on his brutally diminished constituency. For some reason he took a particular, avuncular interest in Blackett. Perhaps he feared for his own mental health in this terrible circumstance.

"She's expected, Sergeant." By seniority of available staff, the man was probably a captain or even police chief for the region, now, but Blackett declined to offer the honorary promotional title. "Drop me off at the top of the street, would you?"

"It's no trouble to take you to the door."

"I need to stretch my legs after the flight."

In the failing light of dusk, he found Clare, almost in shadow, moving like a piece of beautiful driftwood stranded on a dying tide, backward and slowly forward, on his borrowed porch. She nodded, with her Gioconda smile, and said nothing. This evening she wore a broderie anglaise white-on-white embroidered blouse and 501s cut-down almost to her crotch, bleached by the long summer sun. She sat rocking wordlessly, her knees parted, revealing the pale lanterns of her thighs.

"Once again, Doctor," Blackett told her, "you're trying to

seduce me. What do you suppose this tells us both?"

"It tells us, Doctor, that yet again you have fallen prey to intellectualized over-interpreting." She was clearly annoyed, but keeping her tone level. Her limbs remained disposed as they were. "You remember what they told us at school."

"The worst patients are physicians, and the worst physician patients are psychiatrists." He took the old woven cane seat, shifting it so that he sat at right angles to her, looking directly ahead at the heavy brass knocker on the missing CEO's mahogany entrance door. It was serpentine, perhaps a Chinese dragon couchant. A faint headache pulsed behind his eyes; he closed them.

"You've been to the coast again, Robert?"

"I met a dog on the beach," he said, eyes still closed. A cooling breeze was moving into the porch, bringing a fragrance of the last pink mimosa blossoms in the garden bed beside the dry, dying lawn. "He suggested that we've experienced a singularity cataclysm." He sat forward suddenly, turned, caught her regarding him with her blue eyes. "What do you think of that theory, Doctor? Does it arouse you?"

"You had a conversation with a dog," she said, uninflected, nonjudgmental.

"One of the genetically upregulated animals," he said, irritated. "Modified jaw and larynx, expanded cortex and Broca's region."

Clare shrugged. Her interiority admitted of no such novelties. "I've heard that singularity hypothesis before. The Mayans—"

"Not that new age crap." He felt an unaccustomed jolt of anger. Why did he bother talking to this woman? Sexual interest? Granted, but remote; his indifference toward her rather surprised him, but it was so. Blackett glanced again at her thighs, but she had crossed her legs. He rose. "I need a drink. I think we should postpone this session, I'm not feeling at my best."

She took a step forward, placed one cool hand lightly on his bare, sunburned arm.

"You're still convinced the Moon has gone from the sky,

Robert? You still maintain that everyone has gone to Venus?"

"Not everyone," he said brusquely, and removed her hand. He gestured at the darkened houses in the street. A mockingbird trilled from a tree, but there were no leaf blowers, no teenagers in sports cars passing with rap booming and thudding, no barbecue odors of smoke and burning steak, no TV displays flickering behind curtained windows. He found his key, went to the door, did not invite her in. "I'll see you tomorrow, Clare."

"Good night, Robert. Feel better." The psychiatrist went down the steps with a light, almost childlike, skipping gait, and paused a moment at the end of the path, raising a hand in farewell or admonishment. "A suggestion, Robert. The almanac ordains a full moon tonight. It rises a little after eight. You should see it plainly from your back garden a few minutes later, once the disk clears the treetops."

For a moment he watched her fade behind the overgrown, untended foliage fronting this opulent dwelling. He shook his head, and went inside. In recent months, since the theft of the Moon, Clare had erected ontological denial into the central principle of her world construction, her Weltbild. The woman, in her own mind supposedly his therapeutic guide, was hopelessly insane.

6.

After a scratch dinner of canned artichoke hearts, pineapple slices, pre-cooked baby potatoes, pickled eel from a jar, and rather dry, lightly salted wheaten thins, washed down with Californian Chablis from the refrigerator, Blackett dressed in slightly more formal clothing for his weekly visit to Kafele Massri. This massively obese bibliophile lived three streets over in the Baptist rectory across the street from the regional library. At intervals, while doing his own shopping, Blackett scavenged through accessible food stores for provender that he left in plastic bags beside Massri's side gate, providing an incentive to get outside the walls of the house for a few minutes. The man slept all day, and barely budged from his musty bed even after the sun had gone down, scattering emptied cans and plastic bottles about on the uncarpeted floor. Massri had not yet taken to urinating in his squalid bedclothes, as far as Blackett could tell, but the weekly visits always began by emptying several jugs the fat man used at night in lieu of chamber pots, rinsing them under the trickle of water from the kitchen tap, and returning them to the bedroom, where he cleared away the empties into bags and tossed those into the weedy back yard where obnoxious scabby cats crawled or lay panting.

Kafele Massri was propped up against three or four pillows. "I have. New thoughts, Robert. The ontology grows. More tractable." He spoke in a jerky sequence of emphysematic wheezing gasps, his swollen mass pressing relentlessly on the rupturing alveoli skeining his lungs. His fingers twitched, as if keying an invisible keyboard; his eyes shifting again and again to the dead computer. When he caught Blackett's amused glance, he shrugged, causing one of the pillows to slip and fall. "Without my beloved internet, I am. Hamstrung. My preciiiouuus." His thick lips quirked. He foraged through the bed covers, found a battered Hewlett-Packard scientific calculator. Its green strip of display flickered as his fingers pressed keys. "Luckily. I still have. This. My slide rule." Wheezing, he burst into laughter, followed by an agonizing fit of coughing.

"Let me get you a glass of water, Massri." Blackett returned with half a glass; any more, and the bibliophile would spill it down his vast soiled bathrobe front. It seemed to ease the coughing. They sat side by side for a time, as the Egyptian got his breath under control. Ceaselessly, under the impulse of his pudgy fingers, the small green numerals flickered in and out of existence, a Borgesian proof of the instability of reality.

"You realize. Venus is upside. Down?"

"They tipped it over?"

They was a placeholder for whatever force or entity or cosmic freak of nature had translated the two moons into orbit around the second planet, abstracting them from Earth and Jupiter and instantaneously replacing them in Venus space, as far as anyone could tell in the raging global internet hysteria before most of humanity was translated as well to the renovated world. Certainly Blackett had never noticed that the planet was turned on its head, but he had only been on Venus less than five days before he was recovered, against his will, to central Texas.

"Au contraire. It has always. Spun. Retrograde. It rotates backwards. The northern or upper hemisphere turns. Clockwise." Massri heaved a strangled breath, made twisted motions with his pudgy, blotched hands. "Nobody noticed that until late last. Century. The thick atmosphere, you know. And clouds. Impenetrable. High albedo. Gone now, of course."

Was it even the same world? He and the Egyptian scholar had discussed this before; it seemed to Blackett that whatever force had prepared this new Venus as a suitable habitat for humankind must have done so long ago, in some parallel or superposed state of alternative reality. The books piled around this squalid bed seemed to support such a conjecture. Worlds echoing away into infinity, each slightly different from the world adjacent to it, in a myriad of different dimensions of change. Earth, he understood, had been struck in infancy by a raging proto-planet the size of Mars, smashing away the light outer crust and flinging it into an orbiting shell that settled, over millions of years of impacts, into the Moon now circling Venus. But if in some other prismatic history, Venus had also suffered interplanetary bombardment on that scale, blowing away its monstrous choking carbon dioxide atmosphere and churning up the magma, driving the plate tectonic upheavals unknown until then, where was the Venerean or Venusian moon? Had that one been transported away to yet another alternative reality? It made Blackett tired to consider these metaphysical landscapes radiating away into eternity even as they seemed to close oppressively upon him, a psychic null-point of suffocating extinction.

Shyly, Kafele Massri broke the silence. "Robert, I have never. Asked you this." He paused, and the awkward moment extended. They heard the ticking of the grandfather clock in the hall outside.

"If I want to go back there? Yes, Kafele, I do. With all my heart."

"I know that. No. What was it. Like?" A sort of anguish tore the man's words. He himself had never gone, not even for a moment. Perhaps, he had joked once, there was a weight limit, a baggage surcharge his account could not meet.

"You're growing forgetful, my friend. Of course we've discussed this. The immense green-leaved trees, the crystal air, the strange fire-hued birds high in the canopies, the great rolling ocean—"

"No." Massri agitated his heavy hands urgently. "Not that. Not the sci fi movie. Images. No offense intended. I mean.... The affect. The weight or lightness of. The heart. The rapture of. Being there. Or the. I don't know. Dislocation? Despair?"

Blackett stood up. "Clare informs me I have damaged affect. 'Flattened,' she called it. Or did she say 'diminished'? Typical diagnostic hand-waving. If she'd been in practice as long as I—"

"Oh, Robert, I meant no—"

"Of course you didn't." Stiffly, he bent over the mound of the old man's supine body, patted his shoulder. "I'll get us some supper. Then you can tell me your new discovery."

7.

Tall cumulonimbus clouds moved in like a battlefleet of the sky, but the air remained hot and sticky. Lightning cracked in the distance, marching closer during the afternoon. When rain fell, it came suddenly, drenching the parched soil, sluicing the roadway, with a wind that blew discarded plastic bottles and bags about before dumping them at the edge of the road or piled against the fences and barred, spear-topped front gates. Blackett watched from the porch, the spray of rain blowing against his face in gusts. In the distance a stray dog howled and scurried.

On Venus, he recalled, under its doubled moons, the storms had been abrupt and hard, and the ocean tides surged in great rushes of blue-green water, spume like the head on a giant's overflowing draught of beer. Ignoring the shrill warnings of displaced astronomers, the first settlers along one shore-line, he had been told, perished as they viewed the glory of a Ganymedean-Lunar eclipse of the sun, twice as hot, a third again as wide. The proxivenerean spring tide, tugged by both moons and the sun as well, heaped up the sea and hurled it at the land.

Here on Earth, at least, the Moon's current absence some-what calmed the weather. And without the endless barrage of particulate soot, inadequately scrubbed, exhaled into the air by a million factory chimneys and a billion fuel fires in the Third World, rain came more infrequently now. Perhaps, he wondered, was it time to move to a more salubrious climatic region? But what if that blocked his return to Venus? The very thought made the muscles at his jaw tighten painfully.

For an hour he watched the lowering sky for the glow pasted beneath distant clouds by a flash of electricity, then the tearing violence of lightning strikes as they came closer, passing by within miles. In an earlier dispensation, he would have pulled the plugs on his computers and other delicate equipment, unpre-pared to accept the dubious security of surge protectors. During one storm, years earlier, when the Moon still hung in the sky, his satellite dish and decoder burned out in a single nearby frightful clap of noise and light. On Venus, he reflected, the human race were yet to advance to the recovery of electronics. How many had died with the instant loss of infrastructure— sewerage, industrial food production, antibiotics, air condi-tioning? Deprived of television and music and books, how many had taken their own lives, unable to find footing in a world where they must fetch for themselves, work with neighbors they had found themselves flung amongst willy-nilly? Yes, many had been returned just long enough to ransack most of the medical supplies and haul away clothing, food, contraceptives, packs of toilet paper.... Standing at the edge of the storm, on the elegant porch of his appropriated mansion, Blackett smiled, thinking of the piles of useless stereos, laptops and plasma TV screens he had seen dumped beside the immense Venusian trees. People were so stereotypical, unadaptive. No doubt driven to such stupidities, he reflected, by their lavish affect.

8.

Clare found him in the empty car park, pacing out the dimensions of Petra's Great Temple. He looked at her when she repeated his name, shook his head, slightly disoriented.

"This is the Central Arch, with the Theatron," he explained. "East and West corridors." He gestured. "In the center, the Forecourt, beyond the Proneos, and then the great space of the Lower Temenos."

"And all this," she said, looking faintly interested, "is a kind of imaginal reconstruction of Petra."

"Of its Temple, yes."

"The rose-red city half as old as time?" Now a mocking note had entered her voice.

He took her roughly by the arm, drew her into the shade of the five-story brick and concrete structure where neuropharmaceutical researchers had formerly plied their arcane trade. "Clare, we don't understand time. Look at this wall." He smote it with one clenched fist. "Why didn't it collapse when the Moon was removed? Why didn't terrible earthquakes split the ground open? The earth used to flex every day with lunar tides, Clare. There should have been convulsions as it compensated for the changed stresses. Did they see to that as well?"

"The dinosaurs, you mean?" She sighed, adopted a patient expression.

Blackett stared. "The what?"

"Oh." Today she was wearing deep red culottes and a green silk shirt, with a bandit's scarf holding back her heavy hair. Dark adaptive-optic sunglasses hid her eyes. "The professor hasn't told you his latest theory? I'm relieved to hear it. It isn't healthy for you two to spend so much time together, Robert. Folie à deux is harder to budge than a simple defensive delusion."

"You've been talking to Kafele Massri?" He was incredulous. "The man refuses to allow women into his house."

"I know. We talk through the bedroom window. I bring him soup for lunch."

"Good god."

"He assures me that the dinosaurs turned the planet Venus upside down sixty-five million years ago. They were intelligent. Not all of them, of course."

"No, you've misunderstood—"

"Probably. I must admit I wasn't listening very carefully. I'm far more interested in the emotional undercurrents."

"You would be. Oh, damn, damn."

"What's a Temenos?"

Blackett felt a momentary bubble of excitement. "At Petra, it was a beautiful sacred enclosure with hexagonal flooring, and three colonnades topped by sculptures of elephants' heads. Water was carried throughout the temple by channels, you see—" He started pacing off the plan of the Temple again, convinced that this was the key to his return to Venus. Clare walked beside him, humming very softly.

9.

"I understand you've been talking to my patient." Blackett took care to allow no trace of censure to color his words.

"Ha! It would be extremely uncivil, Robert. To drink her soup while maintaining. A surly silence. Incidentally, she maintains. You are her. Client."

"A harmless variant on the transference, Massri. But you understand that I can't discuss my patients, so I'm afraid we'll have to drop that topic immediately." He frowned at the

Egyptian, who sipped tea from a half-filled mug. "I can say that Clare has a very garbled notion of your thinking about Venus."

"She's a delightful young woman, but doesn't. Seem to pay close attention to much. Beyond her wardrobe. Ah well. But Robert, I had to tell somebody. You didn't seem especially responsive. The other night."

Blackett settled back with his own mug of black coffee, already cooling. He knew he should stop drinking caffeine; it made him jittery. "You know I'm uncomfortable with anything that smacks of so-called 'Intelligent Design.'"

"Put your mind at. Rest, my boy. The design is plainly intelligent. Profoundly so, but. There's nothing supernatural in it. To the contrary."

"Still—dinosaurs? The dog I was talking to the other day favors what it called a singularity excursion. In my view, six of one, half a dozen—"

"But don't you see?" The obese bibliophile struggled to heave his great mass up against the wall, hauling a pillow with him. "Both are wings. Of the same argument."

"Ah." Blackett put down his mug, wanting to escape the musty room with its miasma of cranky desperation. "Not just dinosaurs, transcendental dinosaurs."

Unruffled, Massri pursed his lips. "Probably. In effect." His breathing seemed rather improved. Perhaps his exchanges with an attractive young woman, even through the half-open window, braced his spirits.

"You have evidence and impeccable logic for this argument, I imagine?"

"Naturally. Has it ever occurred to you. How extremely improbable it is. That the west coast of Africa. Would fit so snugly against. The east coast of South America?"

"I see your argument. Those continents were once joined, then broke apart. Plate tectonics drifted them thousands of miles apart. It's obvious to the naked eye, but nobody believed it for centuries."

The Egyptian nodded, evidently pleased with his apt student.

"And how improbable is it that. The Moon's apparent diameter varies from 29 degrees 23 minutes to 33 degrees 29 minutes. Apogee to perigee. While the sun's apparent diameter varies. From 31 degrees 36 minutes to 32 degrees 3 minutes."

The effort of this exposition plainly exhausted the old man; he sank back against his unpleasant pillows.

"So we got total solar eclipses by the Moon where one just covered the other. A coincidence, nothing more."

"Really? And what of this equivalence? The Moon rotated every 27.32 days. The sun's sidereal rotation. Allowing for currents in the surface. Is 25.38 days."

Blackett felt as if ants were crawling under his skin. He forced patience upon himself.

"Not all that close, Massri. What, some...eight percent difference?"

"Seven. But Robert, the Moon's rotation has been slowing as it drifts away from Earth, because it is tidally locked. Was. Can you guess when the lunar day equaled the solar day?"

"Kafele, what are you going to tell me? 4 BC? 622 AD?"

"Neither Christ's birth nor Mohammed's Hegira. Robert, near as I can calculate it, 65.5 million years ago."

Blackett sat back, genuinely shocked, all his assurance draining away. The Cretaceous-Tertiary boundary. The Chicxulub impact event that exterminated the dinosaurs. He struggled his way back to reason. Clare had not been mistaken, not about that.

"This is just...absurd, my friend. The slack in those numbers.... But what if they are right? So?"

The old man hauled himself up by brute force, dragged his legs over the side of the bed. "I have to take care of business," he said. "Leave the room, please, Robert."

From the hall, where he paced in agitation, Blackett heard a torrent of urine splashing into one of the jugs he had emptied when he arrived. Night music, he thought, forcing a grin. That's what James Joyce had called it. No, wait, that wasn't it— Chamber music. But the argument banged against his brain.

And so what? Nothing could be dismissed out of hand. The damned Moon had been picked up and moved, and given a vast deep carbon dioxide atmosphere, presumably hosed over from the old Venus through some higher dimension. Humanity had been relocated to the cleaned-up version of Venus, a world with a breathable atmosphere and oceans filled with strange but edible fish. How could anything be ruled out as preposterous, however ungainly or grotesque.

"You can come back in now." There were thumps and thuds.

Instead, Blackett went back to the kitchen and made a new pot of coffee. He carried two mugs into the bedroom.

"Have I frightened you, my boy?"

"Everything frightens me these days, Professor Massri. You're about to tell me that you've found a monolith in the back garden, along with the discarded cans and the mangy cats."

The Egyptian laughed, phlegm shaking his chest. "Almost. Almost. The Moon is now on orbit a bit over. A million kilometers from Venus. Also retrograde. Exactly the same distance Ganymede. Used to be from Jupiter."

"Well, okay, hardly a coincidence. And Ganymede is in the Moon's old orbit."

For a moment, Massri was silent. His face was drawn. He put down his coffee with a shaking hand.

"No. Ganymede orbits Venus some 434,000 kilometers out. According to the last data I could find before. The net went down for good."

"Farther out than the Moon used to orbit Earth. And?"

"The Sun, from Venus, as you once told me. Looks brighter and larger. In fact, it subtends about forty minutes of arc. And by the most convenient and. Interesting coincidence. Ganymede now just exactly looks...."

"...the same size as the Sun, from the surface of Venus." Ice ran down Blackett's back. "So it blocks the Sun exactly at total eclipse. That's what you're telling me?"

"Except for the corona, and bursts of solar flares. As the Moon used to do here." Massri sent him a glare almost baleful in its intensity. "And you think that's just a matter of chance? Do you think so, Dr. Blackett?"

10.

The thunderstorm on the previous day had left the air cooler. Blackett walked home slowly in the darkness, holding the HP calculator and two books the old man had perforce drawn upon for data, now the internet was expired. He did not recall having carried these particular volumes across the street from the empty library. Perhaps Clare or one of the other infrequent visitors had fetched them.

The stars hung clean and clear through the heavy branches extending from the gardens of most of the large houses in the neighborhood and across the old sidewalk. In the newer, outlying parts of the city, the nouveaux riches had considered it a mark of potent prosperity to run their well-watered lawns to the very verge of the roadway, never walking anywhere, driving to visit neighbors three doors distant. He wondered how they were managing on Venus. Perhaps the ratio of fit to obese and terminally inactive had improved, under the whip of necessity. Too late for poor Kafele, he thought, and made a mental note to stockpile another batch of pioglitazone, the old man's diabetes drug, when next he made a foray into a pharmacy.

He sat for half an hour in the silence of the large kitchen, scratching down data points and recalculating the professor's estimates. It was apparent that Massri thought the accepted extinction date of the great reptiles, coinciding as it did with the perfect overlap of the greater and lesser lights in the heavens, was no such thing—that it was, in fact, a time-stamp for Creation. The notion chilled Blackett's blood. Might the world, after all (fashionable speculation!), be no more than a virtual simulation? A calculational contrivance on a colossal scale? But not truly colossal, perhaps no more than a billion lines of code and a prodigiously accurate physics engine. Nothing else so easily explained the wholesale revision of the inner solar system. The idea did not appeal; it stank in Blackett's nostrils. Thus I refute, he thought again, and tapped a calculator key sharply. But that was a feeble refutation; one might as well, in a lucid dream, deny that any reality existed, forgetting the ground state or brute physical substrate needed to sustain the dream.

The numbers made no sense. He ran the calculations again. It was true that Ganymede's new orbit placed the former Jovian moon in just the right place, from time to time, to occult the sun's disk precisely. That was a disturbing datum. The dinosaur element was far less convincing. According to the authors of these astronomy books, Earth had started out, after the tremendous shock of the X-body impact that birthed the Moon, with a dizzying 5.5 or perhaps eight-hour day. It seemed impossibly swift, but the hugely larger gas giant Jupiter, Ganymede's former primary, turned completely around in just ten hours.

The blazing young Earth spun like a mad top, its almost fatal impact wound subsiding, sucked away into subduction zones created by the impact itself. Venus—the old Venus, at least—lacked tectonic plates; the crust was resurfaced at half billion year intervals, as the boiling magma burst up through the rigid rocks, but not enough to carry down and away the appalling mass of carbon dioxide that had crushed the surface with a hundred times the pressure of Earth's oxygen-nitrogen atmosphere. Now, though, the renovated planet had a breathable atmosphere. Just add air and water, Blackett thought. Presumably the crust crept slowly over the face of the world, sucked down and spat back up over glacial epochs. But the numbers—

The Moon had been receding from Earth at a sluggish rate of thirty-eight kilometers every million years—one part in 10,000 of its final orbital distance, before its removal to Venus. Kepler's Third Law, Blackett noted, established the orbital equivalence of time squared with distance cubed. So those 65.5 million years ago, when the great saurians were slain by a falling star, Luna had been only 2,500 km closer to the Earth. But to match the sun's sidereal rotation exactly, the Moon needed to be more than 18,000 km nearer. That was the case no more recently than 485 million years ago.

Massri's dinosaur fantasy was off by a factor of at least 7.4.

Then how had the Egyptian reached his numerological conclusion? And where did all this lead? Nowhere useful that Blackett could see.

It was all sheer wishful thinking. Kafele Massri was as delusional as Clare, his thought processes utterly unsound. Blackett groaned and put his head on the table. Perhaps, he had to admit, his own reflections were no more reliable.

11.

"I'm flying down to the coast for a swim," Blackett told Clare. "There's room in the plane."

"A long way to go for a dip."

"A change of scenery," he said. "Bring your bathing suit if you like. I never bother, myself."

She gave him a long, cool look. "A nude beach? All right. I'll bring some lunch."

They drove together to the small airfield to one side of the industrial park in a serviceable SUV he found abandoned outside a 7-Eleven. Clare had averted her eyes as he hot-wired the engine. She wore sensible hiking boots, dark gray shorts, a white wife-beater that showed off her small breasts to advantage. Seated and strapped in, she laid her broad-brimmed straw hat on her knees. Blackett was mildly concerned by the slowly deteriorating condition of the plane. It had not been serviced in many months. He felt confident, though, that it would carry him where he needed to go, and back again.

During the ninety-minute flight, he tried to explain the Egyptian's reasoning. The young psychiatrist responded with indifference that became palpable anxiety. Her hands tightened on the seat belt cinched at her waist. Blackett abandoned his efforts.

As they landed at Matagorda Island, she regained her animation. "Oh, look at those lovely biplanes! A shame they're in such deplorable condition. Why would anyone leave them out in the open weather like that?" She insisted on crossing to the sagging Stearmans for a closer look. Were those tears in her eyes?

Laden with towels and a basket of food, drink, paper plates and two glasses, Blackett summoned her sharply. "Come along, Clare, we'll miss the good waves if we loiter." If she heard bitter irony in his tone, she gave no sign of it. A gust of wind carried away his own boater, and she dashed after it, brought it back, jammed it rakishly on his balding head. "Thank you. I should tie the damned thing on with a leather thong, like the cowboys used to do, and cinch it with a...a...."

"A woggle," she said, unexpectedly.

It made Blackett laugh out loud. "Good god, woman! Wherever did you get a word like that?"

"My brother was a boy scout," she said.

They crossed the unkempt grass, made their way with some difficulty down to the shoreline. Blue ocean stretched south, almost flat, sparkling in the cloudless light. Blackett set down his burden, stripped his clothing efficiently, strode into the water. The salt stung his nostrils and eyes. He swam strongly out toward Mexico, thinking of the laughable scene in the movie Gattaca. He turned back, and saw Clare's head bobbing, sun-bleached hair plastered against her well-shaped scalp.

They lay side by side in the sun, odors of sun-block hanging on the unmoving air. After a time, Blackett saw the red setter approaching from the seaward side. The animal sat on its haunches, mouth open and tongue lolling, saying nothing.

"Hello, Sporky," Blackett said. "Beach patrol duties?"

"Howdy, Doc. Saw the Cessna coming in. Who's the babe?"

"This is Dr. Clare Laing. She's a psychiatrist, so show some respect."

Light glistened on her nearly naked body, reflected from sweat and a scattering of mica clinging to her torso. She turned her head away, affected to be sleeping. No, not sleeping. He realized that her attention was now fixed on a rusty bicycle wheel half buried in the sand. It seemed she might be trying to work out the absolute essence of the relationship between them, with the rim and broken spokes of this piece of sea drift serving as some kind of spinal metaphor.

Respectful of her privacy, Blackett sat up and began explaining to the dog the bibliophile's absurd miscalculation. Sporky interrupted his halting exposition.

"You're saying the angular width of the sun, then and now, is about thirty-two arc minutes."

"Yes, 0.00925 radians."

"And the Moon last matched this some 485 million years ago."

"No, no. Well, it was a slightly better match than it is now, but that's not Massri's point."

"Which is?"

"Which is that the sun's rotational period and the Moon's were the same in that epoch. Can't you see how damnably unlikely that is? He thinks it's something like.... I don't know, God's thumbprint on the solar system. The true date of Creation, maybe. Then he tried to show that it coincides with the extinction of the dinosaurs, but that's just wrong, they went extinct—"

"You do know that there was a major catastrophic extinction event at the Cambrian-Ordovician transition 488 million years ago?"

Dumbfounded, Blackett said, "What?"

"Given your sloppy math, what do you say the chances are that your Moon-Sun equivalence bracketed the Cambrian-Ordovician extinction? Knocked the living hell out of the trilobites, Doc."

A surreal quality had entered the conversation. Blackett found it hard to accept that the dog could be a student of ancient geomorphisms. A spinal tremor shook him. So the creature was no ordinary genetically upgraded dog but some manifestation of the entity, the force, the ontological dislocation that had torn away the Moon and the world's inhabitants, most of them.

Detesting the note of pleading in his own voice, Blackett uttered a cry of heartfelt petition. He saw Clare roll over, waken from her sun-warmed drowse. "How can I get back there?" he cried. "Send me back! Send us both!"

Sporky stood up, shook sand from his fur, spraying Blackett with stinging mica.

"Go on as you began," the animal said, "and let the Lord be all in all to you."

Clouds of uncertainty cleared from Blackett's mind, as the caustic, acid clouds of Venus had been sucked away and transposed to the relocated Moon. He jumped up, bent, seized the psychiatrist's hand, hauled her blinking and protesting to her feet.

"Clare! We must trace out the ceremony of the Great Temple! Here, at the edge of the ocean. I've been wasting my time trying this ritual inland. Venus is now a world of great oceans!"

"Damn it, Robert, let me go, you're hurting—"

But he was hauling her down to the brackish, brine-stinking sea shore. Their parallel footprints wavered, inscribing a semiotics of deliverance. He began to tread out the Petran temple perimeter, starting at the Propylaeum, turned a right angle, marched them to the East Excedra and to the very foot of the ancient Cistern. He was traveling backward into archeopsychic time, deeper into those remote, somber half-worlds he had glimpsed in the recuperative paintings of his mad patients.

"Robert! Robert!"

They entered the water, which lapped sluggishly at their ankles and calves like the articulate tongue of a dog as large as the world. Blackett gaped. At the edge of sea and sand, great three-lobed arthropods shed water from their shells, moving slowly like enormous wood lice.

"Trilobites!" Blackett cried. He stared about, hand still firmly clamped on Clare Laing's. Great green rolling breakers, in the distance, rushed toward shore, broke, foamed and frothed, lifting the ancient animals and tugging at Blackett's limbs. He tottered forward into the drag of the Venusian ocean, caught himself. He stared over his shoulder at the vast, towering green canopy of trees. Overhead, bracketing the sun, twin crescent moons shone faintly against the purple sky. He looked wildly at his companion and laughed, joyously, then flung his arms about her.

"Clare," he cried, alive on Venus, "Clare, we made it!"

LUMINOUS FISH

WITH PAUL DI FILIPPO

From: The Beadle Monger
To: Local Secundus
Subject: Brane Breakthrough

Let's get this effort on the road. The team has been futzing about far too long. The Faith Gambit pissed itself up against a wall for 3000 local years, and the Science Trope has just about done for them far more quickly. I need a Brane Breakthrough, and I want it now. I suggest you take a closer look at candidate Jeremiah ("Jay") Cornelius, Registered Earth Sentient 2744692043.

From: Local Secundus
To: Lord Beadle Monger
Subject: Brane Breakthrough

Your Eminence, the department has developed a plan for your consideration. Please see Attachment 5338.

From: The Beadle Monger
To: Local Secundus
Subject: Cornelius Brain

Very droll. A pun in their native language, quant suff! Proceed at pace. I want to see a working Messiah before the Galactic Ginnungagap Event closes the Brane Potential Portal.

§

Jay made a beast of himself during dinner. Nobody there except Tim had the faintest interest in the tedious horrors of toiling in the bowels of Henry McKinley's disgusting empire. Least interested of all: long-suffering wife Jessie.

If you don't like working there, man, get another job, she thought but did not say. God knows, she was complicit. They needed the money, and it wasn't going to come from her PhD scholarship. Jessie gazed remotely at her plate, moving a fragment of gristle about the rim. After a time she began to polish her serrated steak knife with a paper napkin. A sort of rough dandruff floated from the napkin to the tablecloth. Annie's glance snared her drifting, absent soul. With a start, Jessie put the knife aside, pushed back her chair, took herself away to the bathroom for a quarter of an hour. Jay, more than half-drunk on Chardonnay, babbled about masturbation magazines and their destruction by free pr0n on the internet.

On the Metra home (at least he hadn't attempted to drive, although he was too mean to call a cab, justifying it by a monologue of dubious ecological reasoning), Jessie bleakly examined the ears of the brown, nodding Eastern European man across from her, next to the door between cars. At the first shrieking corner the door ratcheted, groaned, abruptly found within itself some magical lubricant and sped like a calving one-dimensional iceberg to crash back into its slot. The abrupt jolt was more psychic than physical; it bruised her. She looked at Jay, who was staring in befuddled pleasure at the smeared streetlights, their virtual reality. He failed her gaze. She stood up, pulled angrily at the door. It rolled slightly out of its slot, stuck. On the next curve it crashed fully closed. If the man with the ears had extended his foot into the doorway, Jessie thought, his bones would have been broken by the impact.

They were nothing like a beast's ears. No beast she knew of. The man's head was bald and smooth, regular as some Eastern church's dome. Mosque. At his fringes, the last of his hair was as crimped and curly as, presumably, the hair at his groin. Shit no. On his arms, then. His back. She didn't like him. His feet stuck out into the space where other people might wish to walk, could trip, tumble painfully as the tram turned a corner, might at the very least be obliged to step awkwardly. His ears were very human ears. The ears heard nothing at the moment, of course, because the man was asleep. Was that possible? Asleep on the tram. On the Metra. You can go anywhere within reason. He could easily miss his stop.

"She's certainly a very interesting woman," Jay said.

"How would you know?"

"Know what, precisely?"

Oh, Jessie saw in his mind, you're in one of your moods, are you? One of your incomprehensible, incalculable, unplumbable, fathomless, mysterious, womanly moods. Nothing is as it seems, nothing conveys its own transparent truth.

You prick, she thought.

If the Metra went away all the smeared reds and greens and mercury vapor shapes might be stars floating at the edge of a surging swell, salt at the back of her tongue, endless flowing steppes of grass dark and mysterious and shadowed with beasts with ears like hairy Euclidean theorems, lolling tongues, no doubt, and flowing manes, Christ; and its discontents, its woes, its nasty little mean-spirited toads.

She takes the steak knife from her bag. It has been cleaned to a certain brilliance. The door crashes open again. Jessie imagines taking a single step across the aisle. Jay is watching the night. The cry would be in no language she has ever heard. Hot and wet. Rubbery. It would come free in her hand. The man's eyes open now, staring at her, shifting his feet back under his seat. The train accelerates around a curve and back again. The door crashes and crashes.

Jessie imagines herself holding out the moist ear, a gift really. Jay would watch the man bleeding into his cupped, clawing hand.

"Well, I thought she was interesting," he'd tell her, oblivious.

§

Luminous fish with rubbery lips hung from the heavens, a school of grinning, finny clown-specters. The leader squeaked like a vinyl dog toy, and said, "Jay Cornelius! I will pheromone no Eve girl!"

A dark bird of omen, sharply winged like a stealth killer drone, swooped through the dimming sky and began to gobble the squealing panicky fish with a capacious maw. Without conscious summoning of associations, Jay Cornelius knew this raptor to be an emissary of that beneficent personage known as "the Beadle Monger." Despite its predatory actions, the bird must therefore be doing good.

"I love you," cried Jay Cornelius, laughing joyously. He flung up the heavy Rasta locks from his velvet shoulders. "You are the wind beneath my wigs!"

"You fool." Stately, anfractuous Jimmy Brunner scowled. He descended a sigma sequence, a Planck egg in one hand, his swollen member in the other. "You don't even know what anfractuous means. Think, man."

Slightly embarrassed, Cornelius temporized. "You're right, but let us consider the roots. 'An-' suggests negation. 'Fract-' might be a break, a cleft, a cleavage, a...well, a fracture. So you can't be smashed?"

Now, shielded from any surveillance from the sky, the two men clung together under the bridge, smooching wetly, clasping each the other's gigantic, equine, throbbing manhood. The satisfaction of a climax seemed imminent—

"What the hell?" groaned Jay, waking. A gay Harlequin paperback dream? With babbling fish? And someone absurdly named "the Beadle Monger?" His subconscious was generally as disciplined as a Marine drill sergeant. Why this weird outburst, and why now? And who the fuck was Jimmy Brunner? Nobody he knew, had ever heard of, let alone—

His tongue and the roof of his palate were bone dry: he'd been sleeping with his damn mouth open again. These filthy allergies. His nostrils and eyes were swollen all but shut. The sensation of bristled lips pressing against his still rankled. "Oh my god. That's not me."

Half-dark still, early morning. Turning his head to find Jessie snoring faintly. Continuing to mumble his apologetic credo. "I mean, I swear to god I'm no gay basher, but for fuck's sake—" Under the sheets, he was unequivocally—albeit unequinely—erect. He nudged his wife. She replied in her sleep, "Humph?" and rolled his way. He pushed up her nightie.

"Open to me, my sister, for my need is sore great."

She woke and punched him. "I ain't nobody's sister, jerk, least of all yours. What time is it?"

"Come on, my darling, let me at you. You would not wish to connive in the sin of Onan, I trust?"

"Five minutes only," she said, and gave him a smelly *après le sommeil* kiss.

"Ninety seconds," he promised, "as usual on these occasions," and spat on his fingers. He returned her kiss and caressed her, lathering, heaved up beneath the autumnal covers, entered, plunged, made good his promise, fell back. "Ah my dearest girl. Later for you, I swear. No good deed shall go un...."

"Punished?" But she was falling into sleep again, her own dreams, no doubt, just as full of twisty turns and windings.

"...rewarded," said Jay Cornelius. In a minute he'd get up and check his email and google *anfractuous*. Where does this stuff come from? he asked himself and, remembering then some small part of the vanishing dream, groaned. Jiminy Bullard, was it? Where the hell does it come from? Jessie's damned incessant gender research, maybe.

§

Laughing quietly, Jessie scans into a Word doc a passage from Edmund White's *The Beautiful Room Is Empty.*

I had to put on a leather harness, stick a swan feather up my john's ass, and call him "Pretty Peacock" as he strutted proudly about, cocking his head from side to side like a bird while wanking off in an all too human way. Fifty bucks for me and seventy for Lou who, after all, had organized the party.

She is up to her elbows in unlikely gender research material. These guys do seem to confuse their bodily secretions. On the morning after a rowdy party in the largely gay high rise apartment building where he was living, one New York writer reveals, the elevator floor was awash in urine.

Their own dwelling, hers and Jay's, is on the nose as well, though for less lubricious reasons. After only a week or so of fruitless emails and phone calls ("Okay, lady, she'll be right, see y' soon, sweetheart, oh sorry, look, we'll try for the next clear day, eh?") her builder Robert O'Kelly Branagan, Esq and his jobbie or rather sub contractor, a handsome hunk of bronzed expertise with a powered hydraulic nailing device, named Kyle if such a thing is credible, had appeared at the tolerable hour of 10 a.m. and tore into the roof's shoulder blades with such venom that soon the whole horrid thing lay in splinters in the concrete far below, where she stood at some risk snapping away with her nifty Nikon (as if for a forthcoming article, perhaps in the Tribune lifestyle supplement, on remodeling your inner city Chicago *pied-à-terre*), and a drafty smelly hole was revealed or created through which she cavorted bearing bulging plastic bags, happily quite light, of high thermal capacity mineral wool batts that she helped strew among the rafters, coughing and near to puking owing to quantities of dead birds, molted feathers, old dispersed nests, grime, Neanderthal men's bones and the like. Meanwhile young Kyle was nipping and tucking, sawing and hydraulicking, not a handtool in sight. Art in the age of mechanical reproduction, she thought, and laughed quietly to herself.

§

The meeting that morning with Henry McKinley went poorly for Jay. Miserably, in fact. An agonizing death would be a blessing by comparison. He caught himself. Such a sentiment, he suspected, could be regarded as counterindicative of job satisfaction.

Henry McKinley ruled over the Groper Media empire like Genghis Khan over trampled Eurasia, although with less gentility. The comparison was particularly apt, given Henry's full-blooded Asian heritage—Uighur, to be specific. Adopted and rechristened at a young age by Western parents from the ruins of Urumqi after the Han Chinese had leveled the rebellious city, Henry had grown to nominal adulthood pampered and puffed-up. His native lateral intelligence allowed him to find the easiest path to any selfish goal, and to avoid hard work or any peaks of morality. He had been perfectly fitted to become a magnate in the new style. Today, Groper Media ran a passel of salacious or sensationalistic sites, such as Cunning Runts, Root and Tell, Fork Estate, and Mindlezz Pleazurez. The ad revenue from the gossipy, tawdry, eye-candy-filled venues had bought Henry a yacht (the *Canoodle Canoe*), a beautiful brownstone in Chicago's ritzy Lincoln Park district, a fleet of Lexuses (Lexi? wondered Jay, willy-nilly), and three mistresses, each of a different and complementary ethnicity.

Meanwhile the same enterprise had, over the last five years, provided Jay Cornelius, online editor and all-purpose whipping boy, with sixty-five thousand a year before taxes, a modest house undergoing renovations in Naperville, a monthly pass on the Metra, and all-but-dissertation wife Jessie. The continuance of these benefits relied, naturally, on pleasing Henry McKinley. Which today was just not happening.

Henry's fierce mustachios, cultivated precisely to engender racial memories of Mongol savagery, thus reducing subjects to a jelly-like state, quivered as he addressed Jay. "Have you gone fucking gay on me, Cornelius?"

The hyperbolic and clichéd accusation, merely one of Henry's standard taunts, resonated strangely with Jay today, after last night's disturbing dream. A premonition?

"What makes you say that? I thought the layout for the Taylor Swift and Miley Cyrus spanking session was hot."

"Hot? Yeah—if you were thirteen fucking years old! Who did the photoshopping on that anyhow? A blind monkey with simian AIDS and his head up his ass?"

From the back of the room, an intern named Huddleston timorously raised his hand. "Uh, that would be me, sir...."

"You're out of here. Go to HR and collect your check."

"But, sir, I don't get paid...."

"Then just blow!"

After Huddleston slinked out, Henry turned back to Jay. The hapless editor could feel the eyes of everyone else in the room boring holes of pity, schadenfreude and terror-stoked disaffiliation into his living corpse.

"Cornelius, you're damned lucky not to be following Hudnut out that door."

Am I? thought Jay.

"You know damn fucking well that the only reason anyone visits our sites is because we continually push the envelope of good taste and libel. If we run PG-thirteen pap like this, what will that do to our Google Analytics? True, I intend to run Groper into the ground. But not quite yet, and not with lame ass posts like this. Do you understand now what's expected of you?"

"Yes, sir, I do."

"Well, say it then! What's our fucking *cri de coeur*, man? Our goddamn pole star!"

Jay found the puerile words as unpalatable as fetid garbage, but was forced to utter them anyhow. "Tell it—tell it like it's jizz."

"Fucking ay! Now, get back to work. And get fifty percent more nip slip and camel toe in there!"

Back in his upholstered veal-fattening pen, Jay Cornelius laid his head upon his desk and silently wept for precisely thirty indulgent seconds. Luckily, his back was to the shared aisle and any passersby. When he raised his reddened eyes, the first thing he saw was a picture of Jessie. So he returned to work, ordering a re-shoot of the simulated celebrity catfight with fifty percent more of the mandated lascivious ingredients.

His spirits revived, briefly and somewhat guiltily, on the Metra train home that evening. Usually Jay drowsed, stunned into stupidity and resentment by the day's grotesque demands. Now he opened his weary eyes as a strange rustle went through the car, murmurs and one squeal. A gust of perfume galvanized his allergy-stricken nostrils, and someone dropped into the seat beside him. Jay glanced sidelong, blinked, felt his jaw loosen, looked away, looked back. The young woman ignored his glance. She was fantastically gorgeous. Jay felt his reason totter. Impossible! On an evening Metra route? Wait a minute. It had to be a photo shoot. Vox pop video, something viral for YouTube. He didn't want to be filmed as the sort of idiot who stands behind a celebrity holding up rabbit ear fingers behind her head, so instead he let his eyes shuttle back and forth in search of the AV devices. Doing that he probably looked just as dorkish, he thought in self-reproof. But he couldn't hold his incredulous curiosity back a moment longer. He was a journalist, after all. Sort of. He turned, feeling a fatuous grin on his face, unable to block it, and said, "Excuse me, aren't you—"

"Girly D'joan," the pop diva said wearily. Her voice was electrifying. "Don't tell me your name, bozo, I'm not interested. Frankly, I'm bushed. You want to know why I'm on the Metra instead of coddled with a limousine, but this badge I'm wearing on my left breast which you are far too bourgeois and inhibited to look at declares my allegiance to the principle of Carbon Frugality, which I trust answers your question. Also that guy on the other side of the aisle who looks like a gorilla on steroids? My bodyguard, Slim Harry, and he's packing a taser. Just saying. Have a nice rest of the day." All this canned diatribe, which was surely rehearsed, came at him without a single glance from her famously dazzling icicle eyes. Something slammed into the window. Jay jumped.

"Jesus!"

A smear of dark blood. More thuds. Birds were tumbling from the sky, dozens of them, plummeting in the faded light, hundreds, maybe thousands.

Ms. D'joan gazed impassively past him. "Another avian toxic death event," she murmured to Slim Harry, who'd instantly loomed at her side, protective and immense. "Good thing we took the Metra instead of driving." Multitudes of birds were still flinging themselves at the ground, clanging against steel roof and sides, splattering blood. A window cracked but failed to shatter.

Ahead of the train, rattled by the same suicidal flock, one Sal Travett, behind the wheel of a ten-year-old Kia, tried to slip under the closed gates at a grade crossing and got stuck in the path of Jay's train. The Metra locomotive made short work of Sal and his Kia, but an undetected weak spot in one of the buckling rails caused the car containing Jay, Girly, Slim Harry and a score of other riders to jackknife, punching a metal-edged folding tray completely through Jay's midriff, nearly severing him in two.

§

The Beadle Monger cradled Jay Cornelius's head in its infinitely large, infinitely soft lap, while Jimmy Brunner caressed Jay's fevered brow. "There, there," whispered Jimmy, "it's not as bad as all that. Just take it easy, and you'll soon be whole again."

Jay raised his head up tentatively and looked down upon himself. He was saddened but not surprised to find that he had no body below the neatly truncated waist. He tried to express his feelings about this, but could not speak.

Brunner began softly to sing. "Oh, it's no feat to beat the heat. All reet! All reet! So jeet your seet, be fleet, be fleet—cool and discreet, Honey...."

The warbled lyrics soothed Jay, and he began to relax—until

Jimmy saw fit to administer a cure. The male nurse clutched what appeared to be a grinning moray eel, large around as Jay's forearm. Now he tried to feed it head first down Jay's throat.

Gagging as the eel's snout passed his lips, struggling for breath, Jay rebelled, thrashing futilely without legs, like a character out of a Tod Browning film.

"Cool and discreet, Honey," sang Brunner, as he impossibly threaded the eel down Jay's throat—

§

"Please sit down, Mrs. Cornelius," said the doctor, grave face sunlamp-tanned. "This gentleman is Dr. Hare, our Ethics Officer. Let me offer you—" He pressed an open box of Kleenex toward her side of the desk. Jessie took one, swallowed, blew her nose.

"Ms. Kanavan," she said. "Call me Jessie, Dr. Wu. I want to see Jay. Why won't the bastards let me?"

"Jessie, you do understand that your husband was in the very gravest condition when we began the surgery three days ago. Please let me be blunt. We were obliged to perform what is called a craniectomy—" He broke off, coughed. "Your husband's lower torso was severed almost entirely just below the ribs. Very fortunately, we had a compatible donor, who suffered a massive internal brain injury in the same train accident and whose—"

"God damn it, why didn't you let him just die?" She was weeping again. Bent over, clutching her own belly. It felt torn open.

"Well, you must understand, Ms. Kana—Jessie," the Ethics Officer told her, offended. "The Hippocratic oath. This facility's top surgical team has been preparing for another incident of this kind for five months. Your husband will receive the best—"

"My husband the guinea pig! You're telling me you stitched him onto some dead woman's lower body."

Wu regarded her. "This was a far more serious and complex procedure, Mrs.... Jessie. Fortunately, recent outstanding work with stem cells allows us to anticipate fully functional regrowth of anastomozed neurological structures subserving the—"

"What? What are you babbling about?"

"We originally planned to graft his head to the neck of the donor. That proved infeasible for a number of— In lay persons' terms, Jessie, we transplanted his brain."

She sank back in her chair, faint, ill with horror.

"You fucking shits," she shouted at him. "You've given him a woman's body? What makes you think he'll want to live like this?"

"A rather sexist objection, don't you think, Ms. Kanavan?" said the Ethics advisor.

Jessie was on her feet, enraged, hands extended and clawed, making sounds even she did not recognize as words. Dr. Wu rose, too, made shushing motions with his expert surgical hands. "We have many months of recuperation ahead of us," he said. "You will both adjust. It is a sort of miracle, you know. If this terrible accident had happened anywhere else, your husband would indeed have died within minutes, hours at best. We brought him back from the brink. And that poor woman's death—

"Such a generous donor family!" said Dr. Hare.

"—is not entirely in vain, not now."

§

REPORTER: So what's that shiny thing sticking out of the top of Girly's head? Looks like someone left half a hatchet stuck there.

DR. WU: His head. The patient is Mr. Jay Cornelius. His identity is unchanged. Ms. D'joan is deceased. Let me remind you that the donor's identity is strictly embargoed. It will not be published, and there will be no photographs! You have all signed—

REPORTER: Hey, come on, he's got tits. Great tits.

REPORTER: So've you, Billy. Time to cut back on the Quarterpounders.

(Laughter)

REPORTER: Yeah, but Girly's are better. What a waste.

DR. WU: Gentlemen! And ladies! Please, some decorum. This is a patient who has recently undergone an immensely stressful operation, as the videos you've just viewed demonstrated. Now the fellow from the Post asked about the microwave reflector inserted into the cranium between the two halves of Mr. Cornelius's brain.

REPORTER: It's a Space Age Mohawk!

(Laughter)

DR. WU: What you see is the outer portion of a steel microwave reflector that has been positioned with exacting care to avoid damaging the corpus callosum, which joins the twin hemi—

REPORTER: Keep it simple, doc. We're not all from The New York Times.

(Laughter)

DR. WU: Very well. Let me explain. In simple terms, we had to open the top of the skull to allow the traumatized brain to expand, as it does after injury. In order to effect the transfer without further deterioration, the patient's brain had to be cooled to nearly freezing point, as was explained in the video for those of you who kept up. Now, the stainless steel plate acts as a heat sink and a reflector for the 4GHz microwave—that's 7.5 cm—as well as a temperature control device. Following the Gregory Jones cranial protocol, the microwave beam is collimated with a simple catadioptric collimator, and we use the reflected pi-phase-synchronized microwaves from the central plate to interfere destructively at the center of the brain with the incoming non-reflected beam—

(Noisy hubbub)

§

MEDICAL DIARY OF PATIENT 005: ENTRY #17

Magritte is the prophet of my life. The shards of his broken window, each shattered portion of burst pane thick with the paint strokes of sky, trees, grass, the world; everything ordinary broken yet nothing lost, everything refracted and held, ruined, beneath the raped window. Holograms of indecipherable meaning.

Magritte is the prophet. His bland civil servants falling in eerie quiet through the sweet, undubious sky, bowlered and umbrella'd. Filthy Magritte in his own business suit and the oiled tip of his brush.

The "corporeal face." Do you know that terrible painting, that piercing painting? My portrait. The hair like some damned socialite's winter coat, framing and tumbling about the Face, the Face, the round blind breasts staring back at me below the brow of the shoulders, the unscented nostrils of the navel, that pubic beard with its pursed, hidden mouth, its toothless lacking mouth.... Let's see Jessie cite her fave psychiatrist Lacan when she reads this.

I broke the mirror with my small bloodied fists. They brought the mirror to my room last night and left it here. They told me the time had come to get used to reality. Enough denial. Life is better than death in a ruinous accident. How ungrateful I was to turn my face away from the world to which I had been retrieved with all the surgical skill of wonderful hands cutting open my wrecked cranium and cupping my bloody brain and slopping it into an impossibly handy histocompatible corpse. But nothing is improbable once it's happened. Break down these walls of denial! Implosion therapy, it's called. Beyond a certain point, they implied, coddling has a bad track record. One of their early triumphs, the whispering rumors tell me, found a nail file in her handbag and before they got to her almost had her penis sawed off. Oh God, shit. The fucking feckless bastards.

At least they've taken out the famous "Space Age Mohawk" and screwed my skull back together. Her skull. Nobody mentions her name but I know that face, even with the bandages. Sitting right beside me, poor bitch. Skull itches like a bastard.

Jessie leaves messages every day, comes in two or three times a week. Of course I refuse to see her. Your wife called, they tell me. Your wife. I'd like you to meet Mrs. Jessie Kanavan Cornelius and her wife, Mrs. Jay Girly Cornelius.

The mirrored glass didn't stay on the carpet long enough for me to put any of its slivers into my filthy new body. Clean orderlies. They watch everything through cameras which they make absolutely no attempt to hide. Implosion therapy. Panopticon therapy, Jessie would call it. That damned Frog Foucault. Undoubtedly they'll be pawing through these notes the moment they give me my injection. They'll love that line about filthy new bodies. Stick the injection in. Sleepytime, Jay. Shut eyes. There's a good girl.

§

From: The Beadle Monger
To: All Employees
Subject: Jay Cornelius

I am not pleased. Not pleased at all. You are not trying hard enough. Not by a long shot. I have plans for this one. Large and extensive plans. We all know the drill. A new Messiah is called for upon my favorite test planet, and I am convinced Cornelius has the makings. A certain mundane and self-centered insanity. A perverse genius for creating disturbing new parables of existential unease, longing and dread. A new hybrid physiology. (Very important! Take note!) Wide semiotic bandwidth. Look at him/her, people! What better raw material could I give you to work with!?! It took a hell of a long time for me to set up the plausible concatenation of circumstances, the cascade of bad luck, the woman on the train, the dead birds, all the shit that would make this possible. And you guys are blowing it! Cornelius is slipping away into a funk of self-pity and mordant despair. What happened to the guy who chortled at the luminous fish, and passionately embraced the Brunner eidolon? We need that fellow back in harness!

Let's get that dreamscape romance going again! Fast!

And don't tell me that Unknown Kadath wasn't built in a day!

§

The new drug the nurses gave Jay Cornelius during the second week of his/her post-op mental struggles was one of the recently developed ultrapotent anti-depressives, an acetylcholine uptake enhancer. Irrational and bitter, he/she struggled womanfully against the injection, unfamiliar and undermuscled arms flailing, breasts getting in the way, but was unable to thwart the burly orderlies. The drug was intended to induce a kind of passive state of mental beneficence, but had the unforeseen effect on Jay of rendering him/her utterly flatline, heart as pulseless as a stone, starving cells screaming shrilly.

While the hospital staff rushed about madly with defibrillators and oxygen tanks, and the clinic's spokesperson hastily prepared a worst-case speech, Jay was very busy elsewhere.

Polychromatic water glistened and heaved like billows of luscious, nigh-edible acrylics: goldenrod, magenta, periwinkle. A sun like the Google Chrome logo blazed in the sky. The big luminous fish, hefty as barracuda, were swarming ashore to breed, and the human harvesters of L'Almadrava cove were waiting, spears poised.

Several feet offshore, skirt pulled up and tied between her bare, wet, bronzed legs, white blouse pasted to her nubile breasts, her toes gripping the shifting, sucking sands, Jayne hefted her own pole nervously. Her first harvest. She was only sixteen. Would she comport herself well? The future prosperity of the village rested partially on her shoulders.

A rough male hand dropped upon one of those very shoulders now. As if reading her mind, Jaime Brunelli said, "Your stance is bold, little one. But the angle of your spear lacks a certain, ah, utility. I predict impalement of your own delicate foot upon the first thrust. Here, let me adjust your cast."

Big hairy arms enveloped her, along with the musk of male sweat. Jayne trembled. Jaime Brunelli was one of L'Almadrava's most handsome and desirable bachelors. The fiery way he had danced at the last festival— Jayne found the sea-engendered wetness between her legs taking on new hormonal qualities.

But before she could respond either coquettishly or haughtily to Brunelli's suggestive help, the first battalion of luminous fish were upon them. With a bull-like battle cry, Brunelli disengaged, and Jayne was left on her own.

The first rainbow fish that reached her began to plead for its life, as was the wont of these creatures. It employed a human tongue, but to produce gibberish.

"Beep me the be-bop downlow, sister! Raster the roster! It's a treat to beat my milt on the Missus's eggy strand! Oh, no, don't pierce my male maidenhead!"

Ignoring the siren tones of the fish, using both hands on her hard shaft, Jayne plunged her razored spearhead down and into the fish's back, at just the designated point to sever its spine. Her blow was fine and forceful, and the fish ceased its spasmodic mating dance, beginning a prolonged expiration at her feet like some war captive at the feet of a Roman princess.

"Ai, bonita! I flounder! The word for the world is tuna! Monkey see, sea monkey do!"

Jayne disregarded the pathetic gasps and inane drivel, and continued to stab and slice. Soon, a mound of fishy carcasses surrounded her, putting other victims beyond her reach. Thin fishy sparkling blood threaded the waters in an abattoir's aquarelle. She tried to clamber over the bodies, but only collapsed wearily upon the scaly pile, unaware of time's passing until familiar hands cupped her under her arms (and against her breasts!) and raised her up, totally out of the water.

"My little goddess! Victory is thine! You shined like Venus. No, like Bellona! Your ancestors are grinning in heaven!"

Jayne was suddenly shivering, despite the heat of the day. Instinctively, she wrapped her lithe legs around Brunelli's tree-trunk torso and hugged him to her.

He whispered in her ear. "You were made a hunter today, but I will make you a woman tonight!"

It seemed the interval between the end of the catch and the village celebration in the plaza passed in mere seconds, and when Jayne found herself in the fragrant shadow of a lime tree, kissing Jaime Brunelli with fervid languor, she could sense her destiny unfolding. When he raised her fine skirts and stuck two rough fingers up her wet vagina, she came close to fainting. And when he followed that invasion with the whole rushed length of his thick penis, leaping unleashed from his own gaily decorated trews, she finally did indeed lose consciousness of her whole world.

Jay Cornelius's dream left him/her somewhat gentled, filled with an odd combination of waning remorse, waxing resignation and acceptance, dwindling suicidal impulses, and a barely germinating interest in and excitement about her/his personal future, an emotion tender and crushable as the first pale sprout of a maidenhair fern. Additionally, the brute compulsion of a healing, nicely toned body supplemented the blossoming good spirits. *Was* that earlier dream a premonition?

Lying in bed, she/he poked at the still-vivid memory of life in the fishing village, Jayne's piscine conquests and arboreal defloration. Some sense of eternal recurrence lingered, a lineage larger than himself. Life had gone on in such a fashion since the dawn of human history, for men and women alike, each grappling gender playing their part. Who was Jay Cornelius to fight such immemorial rituals? Just because he had involuntarily switched sides in the old competition, he had no solid right to complain. Happened to a limited number of citizens all the time, at their own instigation. Nip and tuck, fold and invert, extrude and stretch, plump and polish....

Of course he spent some time exploring his new body, as the nerve attachments to his brain strengthened, clarified their renewed identity, pulsed from numbness to dulled medicated aches and twinges and at last into a palette of prods, pinches, strokes, soothing, fondlings. Of course his fingers caressed those fabulous boobs, swept down to touch, titillate, enter the exciting, terrifying complex emptiness where his brain gibbered that his penis should be. But it wasn't like the Jayne dream of fervent lusty girlhood. Yes, there were some of those sensations he'd tried to turn into market fodder for the Groper Media empire and his odious boss McKinley, but mostly it was like trying to tickle yourself. His brain literally didn't know if he was coming or going. If he was Arthur or Martha. He took his fingers away from his vagina and sighed.

At that moment, Jay decided firmly and spontaneously on one simple thing, easily within his/her limited grasp. Pronouns. At least she could be a she. Simplify, simplify, for accuracy's sake and ease of conversation. After all, what mattered more, the meaty mass of corpore or the smaller quantity of mens? Even that organic, formerly male brain was now awash in the female chemicals and hormones this body pumped out, laved by a luteal lake.

And so Jay determinedly became Jayne herself. A certain straining tension immediately evanesced.

Over the next few days her concerned handlers, noting the "progress," let up on the meds and allowed more privileges.

Such as getting attired in loose gray sweats and sitting up in this cheerful, sunny lounge, to receive her first real visitor.

Henry McKinley, togged out even more pavoninely than usual, as if in deference to some imagined girlish heart-flutter susceptibility of his interviewee (Jayne admitted the publisher did carry clothes well), brazened into the lounge with his usual air of bestrider-of-worlds. But Jayne thought to detect, beneath the macho bluster, a layer of nervous uncertainty and ego-failure. Had Henry always radiated this self-denying put-down-ability, or was it something new, engendered by Jayne's unique circumstances?

Oh. My. God. Was this insight a case of feminine intuition coming into play? Faintly suspect. No evident logic. Impossible to spreadsheet. Could be useful, though....

McKinley thrust out something he had carried behind his back. An enormously expensive box of Godiva chocolates. "Take it! Jessie said they were your favorites, even before this titanic fuck-up."

Jayne felt her mouth watering. Nice to see Jayne's body's tastes conformed to Jay's.

This body. The stranger's eyes she hid behind. Who had the donor really been, in Girly's short extravagant life, her legacy of accomplishments and relatives and friends, of dreams and hopes? For the first time since their mutual tragedy, Jayne resolved to think at least a little less about herself and more about the famous young woman she inhabited. Henry pulled up a chair and sat down, his knees almost touching hers. He leaned forward, intruding into her personal space. What an obvious boor! Still, his interest was flattering.

"So you've been talking to Jessie?"

"Damn straight! Couldn't talk to you, could I, lost in that self-pitying fugue. My god, Jay—"

"Jayne."

"Whatever. Don't you realize what you almost threw away

by vegging out and indulging in Britney-Spears-magnitude hissy-fits like that? You are the number one media sensation of the millennium! Or at least of this year. All the other freaks like you who survived—sorry, I mean 'lucky beneficiaries of modern medical wizardry'—have proven hideously unsuitable for inspiring the semi-grossed-out adulation by Joe Sixpack and Jane Soccer Mom. Either the bodies were less than optimally hot, or the brains belonged to rat bastards, or both. The worst case was that embezzling bigamist transplanted into the trailer-park mother of seven. Eeeyeuw! But look at you! A smart, sane guy in a smokin' bod!" Henry paused a moment and looked quizzically at Jayne. "You are still sane, aren't you? No, don't answer that! We can work around anything! Where was I? Oh, yeah, so here you are, with the gifts of the fucking gods in your lap—ha, your lap, that's rich!—and you're like, 'Oh, no, woe is me, I don't have a dick anymore, I miss the old sub-average third leg which I never used anyhow except to dip into the stale wifey once a week tops.'"

Jayne felt a surge of anger at this rude characterization of both her quondam private member and the uses to which it had been put. But then, miraculously, some kind of estrogen-based counter-surge of tolerance and humor overcame the anger, and she smiled.

"Okay, bossman, so I'm incredibly lucky. What about it?"

Henry McKinley held his head as if to prevent it from exploding. "What about it?!? What about it!?! Haven't you been working for me for five years? What did I teach you? Didn't you absorb even a gnat's ass's worth of savvy from me? You are going to assign to Groper Media all representation of you and your incredibly sexy-sad story, and we are going to ride this to fame and fortune and megastar-fuckability. I can say that to you, can't I? You're still Jay Cornelius inside that pretty little head, aren't you?"

"Mostly. But why should I necessarily pick Groper to handle my story? Shouldn't I start a bidding war? Man, this is the body of Girly D'joan! And I'm right here. Talk about an inside scoop!"

Henry seemed genuinely taken aback. "Jayne, do you really think there's anyone out there with more sleaze-marketing expertise than yours truly? This is the story I was born to ride!"

Jayne pondered this honest and unsparing self-assessment. She realized that she no longer hated Henry, but only pitied him. Fuller comprehension of his drives and character had brought tolerance.

"Let me hear some of your marketing plans," said Jayne. "And don't spare the dirt."

§

From: The Beadle Monger
To: All Employees
Subject: Jayne Cornelius

I am highly pleased, highly pleased indeed! Operation Androgyne Messiah is back on track! Big kudos to all relevant departments: creative, fieldwork, grok-meld, scanalytics, sevagram programming and astral bookkeeping. Bonuses to be dispersed according to seniority, with highest senior grades receiving no less than one hundred quanta of karmic fluxion.

Please keep up the good work as we move ahead into the next stages of our campaign of enforced enlightenment.

§

Jayne felt like a hundred million dollars, which was appropriate given yesterday's judicial verdict confirming her sole ownership of all her donor's worldly possessions. This still struck her as an insane decision, but she wasn't complaining. All the usual biometrics declared that she was, indeed, beyond question, Girly D'joan, alive and well and almost fully recovered, her fingerprints and retinal scans and DNA genomic profile unaltered by the dreadful accident. Yes, she now had a different brain, but then similarly, too, all those other transplant patients had grafted kidneys or hearts, and nobody expected them to waive their legal rights of full possession and enjoyment thereof. Henry McKinley had spared no expense in hiring the best law firm and suborning the most pliable judge in Chicago.

But thoughts of wealth and borrowed fame were a distraction. Jayne Cornelius rolled out her Pilates mat, dropped into position, and allowed the energy of oxygen to pass into her blood and tissues. And they were hers now, every cell and corpuscle. Calm, calm. Concentration. Control. Center. Flow. Precision. And the soothing, energizing pulse of breath.

"Jay. Jayne. Christ, sorry, should have knocked." In the doorway, Jessie gazed down at her former husband raised full length from the mat in a Shoulder Bridge, right foot squarely on the floor, perfect left leg raised perfectly in alignment through her elevated torso and hip, left toes pointed like a ballerina's. "My god, Jayne," she said in a tone of confusion, "you're hot, man."

A raw sexual jolt went through Jayne's vagina, roared up her spine, clobbered her diaphragm and lungs en route, brought her to the floor with a crunch. This was nothing like her abortive attempts to touch herself. This was that dream, brought to life—Jaime Brunelli of L'Almadrava. But not a rough, beautiful man from a fantasy. Her wife. Jessie. She felt..wet.

"Come here, you," she said, and rolled to her feet, lithe and poised with the body of a twenty-two-year-old diva. They fell upon each other with hot mouths. After a long raging moment Jessie batted away her hand.

"This is wrong, Jay! You're a girl!"

"I thought you were the expert in gender confusion," Jayne said, withdrawing, pouting despite herself, chagrined. "And what's the probability of that, anyway?"

"It's a popular course," Jessie said. She backed away, found a chair, sat primly, watched her husband, her wife, in that sparkling sequined leotard cut in a lewd slash from her sharp hips all the way down to—"Your lawyer called. Congratulations on the decision."

"Thank you. Jessie, I want you to know that—"

"None of it is mine," she said bitterly. "Yes, your Miss Priss made it very clear. Since you are still legally Ms. D'joan, we're not married and never were. So under the settlement laws of Illinois and indeed everywhere else on the entire planet, I can expect nothing, not a penny."

"Hey, hey, baby." Jay surged up inside Jayne. "You'll have everything you need, and more. This...my donor, she was loaded. Is loaded. If I never sing another song for her, she'll be rich until we both die."

"She's already dead. Or you are, whatever."

"You and me, I meant. I told Jesus to write you a check for a million and a half and have it ready for you at the office.' She pronounced it in the Hispanic fashion, Hay-soos. "Didn't you—"

"Who's Jesus?"

"Jesus Saves." Sah-vays. In a happy moment, like the past of their marriage instantly recovered, Jessie blinked and her eyes rolled.

"You're shitting me. You have a money manager named Jesus Saves?" Anglo pronunciation.

Jayne burst out laughing, and felt the tension fall away from her tensed shoulders. The Pilate mat was calling to her. "Right. Right. Man, it's just one crazy coincidence after another."

She found a chair and kicked it closer to her wife. Ex-wife. Widow. Whatever. She reached out both hands and after a moment's pause Jessie took them. "Babe, this is too crazy. But I'm taking steps right away to deal with one issue." Jayne took a deep breath, let the dreams flood through her. Something was trying to tell her something, that was sure as shit. Jay no more. Cornelius no more, either. Time to roll the dice and start over. "I'm changing my name."

"You already changed your name." Now Jessie was stroking her right hand as if it were a small child's, or perhaps a kitten. "Let me guess. Um. Darby N. D'joan?"

"Ha ha." Some old movie they'd seen together? No, an eighteenth century poem Jessie had studied in her gender crimes course, wasn't it? The weather-beaten old couple who'd stayed together through thick and thin. "Sorry, not any longer, sweetheart. This thing that's happened to me, I tell you, someone up there either likes me or hates me, and I don't know which it is, yet. But I got stuck here in this gorgeous bod for a reason, Jessie. Maybe I'm some kind of message to the world."

"Oh shit, Jay." Her widow dropped her hand. "Don't tell me you got religion. It just was an accident, and then a bunch of medical ghouls used you for an experiment. I know, sorry, that was uncalled for, you've recovered beautifully, but...." She trailed off. After a moment she said, "So what's the new name?"

"Jayne Brunner." The person in Girly D'joan's living corpse stood up, squared her shoulders, felt the still-unfamiliar weight of her breasts as they shifted under the lycra.

"Well, whatever. So are you now Mrs. Brunner or Ms. Brunner, Jay?"

"Neither." She offered her widow a vulpine display of teeth, and led her toward the door. "I'm an old-fashioned girl, it seems. Call me Miss Brunner."

§

Somewhere behind the multiverse, the Beadle Monger experienced a small frisson. The Eidolon Lure had been taken.

A Glaroon nodded in satisfaction."Now to nudge the human's Messiah Complex into overdrive, Beads."

"Yes indeed. 'Miss Brunner'," they muttered to itselves. "Now that sounds...quite promising."

For Mike Moorcock and Jerry Cornelius

COMING BACK

Yes, by now he admits that Jennifer is not deliberately driving him crazy. Quit laying it on her, Rostow chides himself. His Bastilled lunacy is self-evidently self-inflicted. There can be no doubt, as Tania had always insisted, that his is a personality gruesomely at risk, pumping through spasms of mania and depression, elation and reproach. As he glances up, the bulwarks of censure shear free of their hinges. The three coil techs, finishing up, share his appreciation with ogles and grins.

Descending the worn rubber treads of the catwalk, its nonmagnetic structure faintly creaking and sronging in ludicrous counterpoint, Jennifer's legs are golden with undepilated summer hairs. Certainly he will lose his reason. It is her innocent, unconscious hauteur that propels Rostow's intolerable aspirations.

Who would believe that less than three weeks ago, governed by hard liquor and soft drugs, his hands had crept like pussycats over those shins, pounced past her knees to her thighs and beyond, while all the while dexterous Auberon Mountbatten Singh, D. Sc., coolly worked at the far end of her torso with mysterious expertise, soothing her brow, the edges of her jaw, the latent weakness at her throat, the revealed swell of her breasts? Even at this moment Rostow can scarcely credit his role in that maniacal and tasteless contest. Was it a contest? As she steps from the catwalk to her computer terminal, Rostow groans at an ambiguity only he perceives.

If even once she took stock, fixed him with, say, a single

killing glance of rebuke and rejection...that would put an end to it. He might flail himself definitively and be done. Instead, she moves with languid competence in his marginal survival spaces like a neutrino beam wafting through a mountain of solid lead.

"Hi," she offers, settling herself in a molded seat. Her gaze penetrates him for an instant, moving after a beat to her keyboard. "Stan's on his way with the entire entourage. I spied."

"*Jambo*," says Rostow. It's all there, bolted into his larynx. Dutifully he runs the coded sequence of knobs and toggles which shunts the system from Latent to Standby. He nods to the departing technicians. There is a Parkinsonian tremor in his stupid fingers. "Pouring spirits down their throats, I guess. Softening them up."

Neat square indicators simmer vividly as the control instrumentation, swift bleats from his console to hers and back, patch into readiness. "This little number should sober them," she observes. "'*Jambo*'?"

"Swahili for 'Hello, sailor'." A thread of mush in his voice and his brain tells his ear that the inflection was wrong. I blew it. Every time I blow it. With a mental fist he clouts his forehead. There is no time for limping second guesses. Stan Donaldson's abrasive voice precedes the man by half a second as the door swings wide for the expensive feet of the Board of Directors.

"We acquired it from Princeton, Senator," the department head is saying. "ERDA paid out a quarter of a billion dollars for a Tokamak Fusion Test reactor that was obsoleted overnight when Sandia secured sustained fusion by inertial confinement."

It seems to Rostow, squinting from the side of his eye and jittery with alarm, that this approach is a mistake. The senator is notorious for his loathing of costly obsolescence. Uh-huh. Buonacelli halts in midstride, pokes a finger into Donaldson's chubby chest. "Another sonofabitch Ivy League boondoggle. By the Lord, that's the kind of crap I won't abide."

Donaldson stands his ground. His own rasp is melodic after

the senator's gravel hurtling from a tip-truck.

"Their blunder was our good fortune, sir," he says. "They were going to haul off the toroidal coils for recycling, but I managed to have them diverted to this laboratory. Everything is surplus or off-the-shelf. It made for a considerable saving."

Somewhat mollified, Buonacelli pushes forward to loom over Jennifer Barton's supervisor terminal, his minnows in attendance. "I'm still god-damned if I know what your magnets are for. Come straight out with it, man. The trustees won't be slow to scrap any project that smacks of self-indulgent tinkering." The set of his agribiz frame shows approval of Jennifer at least. "Convince us, and fast. This is the third department we've been dragged through today, and my feet are killing me."

"Miss Barton, could you fetch the senator a chair?"

Incredulous on her behalf, Rostow burns. Buonacelli holds the woman's biceps as she rises. "That's fine, honey, I'll stand." An arm goes around her shoulders in a friendly squeeze nobody in his right mind could construe as avuncular. Eddie Rostow damages his tooth enamel. "Don't bother buttering me up, Dr. Donaldson. Let's get straight to the meat. What does this pile of junk do? Why do you deserve more megabucks?"

Rostow's chagrin buckles to delight as Stan's moist, unhealthy jowls darken. No doubt this will be the third or fourth time Donaldson has tried to explain the advanced-wave mirror to the accountants. Probably, Eddie decides, Buonacelli is just baiting him. The old bastard might know zilch about high-energy physics, but he's nobody's fool.

There again, it would serve Donaldson right if they haven't followed a word he's been saying. The man revels in pretentious jargon. Rostow hears a scurry of furry feet in the cardboard box near his own, cranes his neck, breaks up in silent mirth. The white bunny rabbit in the box is making its own critical observations. Cottontail high, it's dropping a stream of dry pellets into the shredded lettuce that litters the box.

Florid, Stan has decided to simplify his spiel. He's saying:

"A totally new branch of technology, gentlemen, Perhaps my previous remarks were overly technical."

"New like Princeton?"

"New like Sandia," the professor says, grasping thankfully at the straight line. "Yet thoroughly rooted in classical theory. What we have here, gentlemen, is the answer to a puzzle provoked by James Clerk Maxwell more than a century ago. Maxwell," he glosses, "was the genius who first showed that electricity and magnetism were one and the same. His equations are the basis of all electronic technology."

"For history we fund historians," one of the committee says coldly, currying favor, and recoils slightly when Buonacelli growls.

Irritated and emboldened, the great physicist states loftily: "Physics is precisely the accumulated history of great physicists. My point, Senator, is that Maxwell's equations for electromagnetic wave motion have two sets of solutions. One set describes what we term *retarded* waves, where fluctuations are broadcast outward due to the acceleration of a charged particle. Radio waves from a transmitter are retarded waves, akin to the ripples from a stone dropped in a pond."

Rostow monitors surges of power in the system, holding it in equilibrium. He seeks Jennifer Barton's eye, hoping for a shared long-suffering grimace, but her attention is directed to the listening senator.

Donaldson is creeping into pomposity again. "The other solutions, equally valid in theoretical terms, we call *advanced* waves. Until now they have never been detected, let alone utilized."

"Radio waves get drawn back into a transmitter?" Buonacelli poses acutely, puzzled.

"Exactly." Donaldson rewards him with a satisfied pout. "Advanced waves converge to a point. Another way of looking at it is to say that they travel backwards in time. They put time into reverse. Normally, for complex reasons, the two sets of waves interfere, yielding no more than the retarded component. What I've done here with this equipment—"

Unnoticed, Eddie Rostow sits bolt upright and his face distorts in a throttled shriek. What *you've* done, you thieving sonofabitch?

But Buonacelli's scandalized roar has filled the lab. Suddenly it is obvious that indeed he had not grasped the earlier explanations. "Who in hell do you think you are, Professor—H. G. Wells? Don't you ever learn? How dare you stand there and shamelessly tell us you've been spending the university's endowment on a *time* machine? Credit me with the sense I was born with."

As Rostow spins in his chair, the dignitaries are stomping toward the door. Before Donaldson finds words, Jennifer Barton has magically slipped into Buonacelli's path. "Surely you're not leaving yet, Senator? Won't you at least wait for the demonstrations we've prepared for you?" She blinks as if something is in her eye.

"Harrumph!" Buonacelli lifts her hands in his beefy paws. "I don't know how they've taken you in, my dear. Never trust a scientist. If they're not lunatics, they're swindlers. Either way, it's a waste of good tax revenue."

"Why, Senator! I'm a scientist myself."

He releases one hand, strokes his jaw. "My apologies, dear lady. To tell the truth, my eldest son is a chemist at Dow." Gallantly he bows, retaining one of her hands. "Very well, gentlemen. To please this charming lady, let's take a look at the professor's so-called demonstration."

Wincing, Rostow spins quickly back to his station. He knows he'll be the butt of Stan's fuming humiliation the moment the directors are on their way. Why do I put up with it?

Tersely, the professor tells Buonacelli, "You may examine this equipment thoroughly." He leads them to the mirror chamber buried between gigantic doughnut-shaped magnets, slides open the weighty hatch. With heavy sarcasm he says, "Assure yourselves it's quite empty. There are no hidden trapdoors or disappearing rabbits." Rostow swallows a snigger, his eye on the white bunny munching in its box between his feet. Poor little beast, he thinks an instant later. I hate that part of it. But it's going to rock Buonacelli on his heels and open his wallet.

"Advanced waves are generated in every molecular interaction. Within

these confines they are reflected almost totally. The crystalline surface of the chamber constitutes an *array* of laser-like amplifiers which augment the advanced-wave component." My idea, Eddie Rostow wants to shout. Without that, you'd have a big magnetic field going absolutely nowhere. But whose name will go on the paper? He says nothing. Donaldson puts his head inside the chamber. Dully, as he twists back and forth, his muffled voice states: "As you see, it's perfectly safe at the moment." An almost irresistible impulse floods Rostow. Regretfully, he pulls his finger back from the power switches.

"Okay," growls Buonacelli, "it's empty. So?"

Jennifer Barton leaves her terminal and returns with a flask of boiling water in one hand and a tray of ice cubes in the other.

"This will be simple but graphic, Senator," she says. It is Stan's notion of theatrics to have her fetch the props. "As you can see, this water is very hot. Would you care to dip in your pinky to test it, sir?"

"Thank you, honey, but I guess I recognize hot water when I see it."

A crony adds, unnecessarily, "You've been in plenty of it in your time." Everyone laughs ingratiatingly. Jenny drops two large ice cubes into the flask, places it inside the chamber. She goes at once to her terminal, and her features blank out in the inert Zen concentration of perfect egoless programming. The assembled company stare foolishly at the sight of two ice cubes slowly dissolving. Donaldson dogs the hatch. An enhanced but rudimentary image of the interior comes to life on an adjacent TV screen. It shows two ice cubes slowly dissolving.

"Ideally," the professor says, fists clenched at his sides, "the chamber would be absolutely shielded. We've sacrificed some signal purity so you can see what's going on inside. The process will still work reasonably well. Is the system on-line, Eddie?"

"Yeah." Rostow's own palms are wet. The whole performance is premature. Five successful tests and two fails. Donaldson's a yo-yo, bobbing from an obsession for publicity at any cost through close-mouthed paranoia and back. It'd almost be nice if the damned thing blew out. Bite your tongue. It's my baby. Go, go.

"Well, don't just sit there."

"Right, Stan," says Rostow through his teeth, and smashes the toggle closed.

There is no new sound, no deep shuddering hum or rising whine. Current in the magnetic coils goes to fifty thousand amps, and there is a faint creaking as monstrously thick non-magnetic structural members crave one another's company in the embrace of the stupendous field. Sometimes, with the lights dimmed, Rostow has seen phantom bars of pale light crossing his line of sight. Field strengths of this magnitude can screw with the visual cortex. Or maybe the magnets bend cosmic radiation through the soft tissues of his eyeballs and brain, nibbling tiny explosions of pseudolight in his synapses. It isn't happening now. Everyone stares at the TV monitor, waiting for something apocalyptic. Caught by the mood, Rostow abandons his console and steals across to join them.

"I'm still waiting," Buonacelli barks.

"Watch the ice cubes. Senator," Jennifer tells him.

"Dear God." It is one of the accountants who first grasps what is happening. "The bastards are getting bigger!"

"Just so," Donaldson says, loosening his fists. "The basic conservation law: heat can't pass from a cold object to a hot one. But time inside the mirror is now running backwards, gentlemen, for all practical purposes. Advanced Maxwell radiation, amplified by the lasing action, is converging on the flask.

The Second Law of Thermodynamics is repealed."

Rostow's body thumps to his pulse. Steam is rising once more from the flask. A pair of unblemished cubes jounce at the surface of the boiling water.

"Fantastic," Buonacelli groans. "I take it all back. Dr. Donaldson, this is the wonder of the age."

"You have yet to witness the more dramatic part of our demonstration." Turning abruptly, the professor stumbles into Rostow. "Wouldn't it be better if you were at your console, Eddie? Please power the system down immediately and put it on Standby. Where's that animal?"

Rostow chews at part of his face. "I'll get him for you." He slouches in his seat, runs the current down, feels in the box with his left hand for the bunny. Helplessly he glances at Jennifer Barton. She is watching him. Fingers tight around the bunny's ears, he hoists it from the box and feels acid in his stomach as he identifies the flash of emotion in her face.

Taking the bunny, Donaldson suggests: "Remove the flask and then stand by for my mark." Rostow seethes, but welcomes the distraction. Behind him the bunny squeals. Nothing wrong with its memory at any rate. There's a meaty thunk. When he turns back with the remelted cubes, Rostow finds the professor marching toward him with the bunny's bloody, guillotined corpse in a sterile glass dish. One of the accountants, no great white hunter, is averting squeamish eyes. Buonacelli's are narrowed in wild surmise.

Resurrection is at once prosaic, electrifying, impossible to comprehend. On the monitor, the bunny's grainy sopping fur lightens as untold trillions of randomly bustling molecules reverse their paths. As the flow staunches, its poor partitioned head rolls upward from the glass bowl and fits itself seamlessly to its unmarked neck. Prestidigitation. The bunny blinks spasmodically, slow lids snapping upward, wiggles his ass, and disgorges a strip of unchewed lettuce. The lab thunders crazily with applause.

"By the Lord, you're a genius!" Color has drained from

Buonacelli's seamed features; it surges back, as he beats Donaldson's shoulders. "Reviving the dead...." He pauses and adds slowly, with avaricious appetite: "A man could live forever."

"I doubt it," Rostow tell him. "We can put people back together, and heal wounds. But unfortunately it won't help those who die of natural causes."

"Rejuvenate them!"

"It'll rub out your memory."

"Not your financial holdings, by God." The senator flexes his fingers, thickened by incipient arthritis. "Plenty of memories I could happily live without. You could brief yourself—leave notes, tapes...."

"Sorry. Reversed time passes at the conventional rate. Do you want to spend forty years in solitary confinement? Besides, even the immensely rich couldn't run this machine nonstop for that long."

Donaldson is nodding his agreement, until it occurs to him that he's no longer the center of attention. "I did ask you to stay at your console, Eddie. Miss Barton, thank you, that will be all today." With smiles all around, he ushers the committeemen away from the mirror into a cozy space of his own contriving. Eddie Rostow watches them troop toward the door. They remain in shock, their several minds no doubt working like maniacs as each tries to figure himself in and the rest out. "Truly astounding," one says as the door closes.

Rostow covers his face. In the huge empty lab he hears Jennifer Barton rise from her seat. He opens his fingers for a peek. She is regarding him across her deactivated terminal; he cannot read her expression with certainty. Once more he covers his eyes and listens to the tap of her shoes, the click of her exit. Wistfully he sniffs the air for a trace of her scent, more natural pheromone than applied cosmetic. On the monitor screen, the bunny is scratching at the walls of the mirror chamber. Poor little beast. Dazed by anger, lust, remorse and sympathy, Rostow strides to the chamber and plucks the bunny to freedom and mortality.

A dizzying aura of bloody light spangled with pinpoints of imploding radiance momentarily blinds him. "Cretin," he mouths, dropping the rabbit and slamming the hatch. He runs toward the console, clutching his eyes, and barks his shin on the back of his chair.

Nothing explodes. When his vision clears he scans the bank of square lights on the system he had left running at full power without computer supervision. Christ Almighty, we need a fail-safe on that. Who'd expect anyone to be so dumb? Shuddering, he runs through the step-down with scrupulous attention to detail, double-checking every item.

As he finishes, he notes the bunny lumping near his numb toes, trying to get back into its box. The stupid bastard is hungry again. He heaves it in.

The afternoon is only half done. This is insane. Did Roentgen finish off his full day's work after the first exhibition of X-rays? Surely Watson and Crick didn't quietly mop up the lab after they'd confirmed the DNA helix. I'll take myself off and tie one on, he decides. I'll get drunk as a skunk. He'd done just that after the first successful trial of the advanced-wave mirror: alone, bound to secrecy by his nervous department head, he'd sat in a downtown bar and poured bourbon into his belly until the trembling urge to howl with joy dopplered into a morose blur. And paid for it next day. Oh, no, not that again. I'll march down to Jennifer's room and lay it all out for her. Invite her to a movie, a plate of *Fricassée de Poulet* at Chez Marius and a bottle or two of Riesling. We'll get smashed together, bemoan Donaldson's bastardry; hell we'll leave Donaldson out of it; we'll go to her apartment and screw our tiny pink asses off.

His hand had been all the way up her skirt, and the next day she'd acted as if nothing had ever passed between them. Did goddamned Auberon Mountbatten Singh have his evil Anglo-Indian way with her that night, rotating through ingenious positions? It doesn't bear thinking about.

For a moment, to his horror, Rostow finds himself regretting his divorce. Worse, he finds his baffled free-floating lust drifting in the direction of the image of his ex-wife. Swiftly, before he damages his brain beyond repair, he puts a stop to that

With effort he levers up from the dead console and mooches to the foot of the catwalk, leaning on its handrail. I have to stop brooding about Jennifer. I could have killed myself shoving my hand into the powered mirror, through the temporal interface. I do not interest her strangely. Undoubtedly only fantastic self-restraint prevented her from smashing my impertinent jaw with her knee. My god, how can I look her in the eye?

This kind of maundering unreels through Rostow's head until he is so bored with it that he turns back to check the data for tomorrow's log of tests. Glancing at the wall clock, he sees that he's wasted half an hour in useless self-laceration. Maybe, after all, he should simply run out the door, burst into her office, and screw her until the sweat pops from her admiring brow. Oh my God. He drags a heavy battered mathematical cook-book from the bench where the bunny rabbit was murdered and resigns himself to the honorable discharge of his employ-ment. A dizzying aura of bloody light spangled with pinpoints of imploding radiance momentarily blinds him. "Cretin," he mouths, dropping the rabbit and slamming the hatch. He runs toward the console, clutching his eyes, and barks his shins on the back of his chair.

Nothing explodes. A startled, unconvinced element in his mind asks itself: Hasn't this all happened before?

He notes the bunny lumping near his numb toes trying to get back into its box. The stupid bastard is—Oh Jesus. A small disjointed part of him watches the wind-up golem, as detached as the bunny's head after its sacrifice. This isn't *deja vu*. It's too sustained. I'll take myself off and tie one on, he decides. I'll get drunk as a skunk. Oh my God, I'm tracking through the same temporal sequence twice. But that's truly insane, delu-sional. Time isn't repeating itself. I'm using the advanced-wave mirror system as a metaphor, at some profoundly cracked-up level of my unconscious. Didn't my dear sweet brilliant wife complain that I'm a cyclothymic personality, a marginal manic-depressive, obsessively driven to repeat my laments? I've careened into a rut. A conditioned habit of thought. Jennifer Barton is driving me nuts. I can't even see her in the same room without brooding on the same stupefying regrets and fantasies. I'll march down to Jennifer's room and lay it all out for her. Invite her to a movie, a plate of *Fricassée de—*

All his sensations are scrambled. The terror in his head clangs against the lugubrious mood of his hormones. I looked at the clock, he tells himself desperately, clutching for a falsifiable test. Sound scientific method. What did it say? 4:37. Last time round. He grips that single datum, while his mutinous corpse leans on the railing of the catwalk, one foot propped on a rubber tread. Glancing at the wall clock, he sees that he's wasted half an hour—

Oh God Almighty. 4:37. Exultation bursts in his mind, leaving his flesh to plod like lead. Hold it, that doesn't mean you haven't flipped your cranium. Everyone has a built-in clock. Three Major Biorhythms Ordain Your Fate, that sort of thing. He wants to giggle, but his chest and jaw don't respond to the wish. His frail flesh has resigned itself to the honorable discharge of his employment. A dizzying aura of bloody light spangled with pinpoints of imploding radiance momentarily blinds him.

No! the small anarchic part screams silently. I can't stand it. It's happening again. I'm stuck in a loop of time. Wait, I can prove it. I dropped the rabbit. Any moment now I'll glance down and see it....

...trying to get back into its box. The stupid bastard is hungry again. He heaves it in—

Rostow tells himself: this is the third time round. Or is it? Were he in control of his programmed muscles, he would shudder. Maybe I've been caught in this loop for all eternity, or at any rate long enough for random quantum variations in one part of my brain to set up an isolated observing subprogram.

Jesus, how much pseudo-duration would that take? Ludwig Bolzmann's *Stosszahlansatz* postulate: ordered particles spontaneously decay into chaos, but given enough interactions they can swirl together again into a new order, or even the old order. Suppose I'm at the bottom of a local fluctuation from unordered equilibrium. What's the Poincaré recurrence time for a human being and his lab? Say ten to the tenth power raised to the thirtieth power. That's *absolutely* grotesque. The entire universe would have evaporated into dead cold soot. So I'm recycling. I stuck my mitt in the hatch and screwed up the mirror. I'm looping through the same 30 minutes forever, knowing exactly what's due next and unable to do anything about it. Maybe I'm not crazy—but I will be soon.

I'm a prisoner, Rostow realizes, in my own past.

For a moment, to his horror, he finds himself regretting his divorce. Worse, he finds—

Hold it, the isolated segment thinks. If I'm patched into the lasing system, the additional mass of my body is pushing the mirror into a singularity on an asymptotic curve, tending to the limit at 30-odd minutes duration. But Hawking has shown that quantum effects re-enter powerfully under such conditions. After all, Rostow debates with himself, they must, or I'd be unaware of what's happening. The human brain has crucial quantum-scale interactions. Hadn't Popper and Eccles been arguing that case for years? So maybe I can break free of my prior actions. What's to stop me *deciding* to cross the room and pick up the flask from the bench where I put it?

Jenny, you bitch, he thinks, why are you doing this to me? Bitterly, he wanders to the bench and lifts the lukewarm flask of melted ice-cubes to his lips. It tastes terrible. He puts it down with revulsion, then picks it up once more and stares in amazement. I'm not thirsty. Something *made* me do that—

—the flask slips out of his fingers and shatters. The twin sectors of consciousness fuse.

Eddie Rostow goes stealthily to his console chair and lowers himself with infinite delicacy.

Aloud, he mutters: "I'm not out of it yet. Or am I? Is one change in the cause-and-effect sequence sufficient to take me off the loop?" Mellowing afternoon light slants across his fists from the barred skylight, a sympathetic doubling to the shadow from harsh white fluoros, and his voice echoes wanly. Rostow flushes. If Donaldson comes through that door to hear him mumbling to himself—

But that isn't on the agenda, is it? If anyone in the entire world has a certified lease on his own immediate future, it's Edward Theodore Rostow, doctoral candidate and imbecile. The sparkling impossible conjecture has come belatedly on tiptoes to smash him behind the ear. With a glad cry he leaps to his feet. "I can do anything! *Anything* I wish!"

I'm not trapped. I thought I was a prisoner, but I'm the first man in history to be genuinely liberated. Set free from consequences. *Do it.* If you don't like the results, scrub it on the next cycle and *try again.*

Rostow grabs up paper and calculator, scrawls figures. Start by establishing the exact parameters. See if the loop is decaying or elongating. It's aggravating, but he rounds out the cycle with his eyes clamped to the clock. The bloody aura flashes a half-minute after the digital clock jumps to 4:37. With iron control he keeps hold of the rabbit and wrenches his head around as vision clears. Three minutes after four. His endocrine fluids are telling him to panic, sluggishly stuck in the original sequence. Rostow's excited mind shouts them down. Denying the inertia of previous events, he takes the wriggling bunny to his console and places it carefully in its cardboard home. A thirty-four minute loop, forsooth.

Considerable effort is required initially. Rostow's First Theorem, he thinks, grinning. Any action will continue to be repeated indefinitely unless a volitional force is applied to counter that action. Fortunately, the energy necessary to alter intention and will is in the microvolt range. Yes. The brain *is* a quantum machine for making choices, once you understand that choice is possible.

He halts with his hand on the door latch. Think this through. Stan Donaldson, esteemed head of department and professor, is the last sonofabitch who deserves to know. Will I fall off the loop if I wander away from the mirror? Leaving the loop is suddenly a most undesirable prospect. Yet some obscure prompting dispels these trepidations. Rostow opens the door and enters the long colorless corridor.

Led by bombastic Donaldson, the Board of Directors is taking the stairs to the free hooch. Jennifer Barton's thick mane swirls as she shakes her head, freeing her arm from the senator's grip. On the bottom step she pivots and turns right, toward her small office in the Software Center. Not celebrating? Eddie shuts the lab door and pursues her down the corridor.

I can't tell her about it. She'd be obliged to call for the men in white. Up ahead, she slips into her office without looking in his direction. Arousal stirs in him, fecklessly.

Not truly believing it, he reminds himself: Anything is possible. There are no payoffs. The world's a stage, tra-la. "I'll just lay it on the line," he mutters seriously. A passing student blinks at him. With an inane giggle, Rostow nods. Loudly, in a crisp tone, he tells the student: "I'll ask her what the hell it is between us."

"Oh," says the student, and walks on, swiveling his brows.

High out of his gourd on freedom unchecked by restraint, Rostow zooms toward joy with the woman of his dreams. In a magical slalom on the vinyl tiles, he bursts through Jennifer Barton's door and thrusts his hands on the desk's edge. Her lab coat lies on a filing cabinet; she stands at her window, brushing her hair. "Tell me, for Christ's sake," Eddie barks before his vocabulary can freeze up, "what the hell it is between us."

His secret sweetheart narrows her eyes. With deflated, acute perception, Rostow surmises that perhaps he is not *her* secret sweetheart. "I hate it with the rabbit," she tells him, putting the brush in a drawer. "But it was a sensational *coup de théâtre*. Coming up for a drink?"

"Didn't you notice? I wasn't invited."

"Surely it was understood." She is being patient with him. Rostow closes the door at his back and sits on the desk. Stress is winding him tight. Has the stoned euphoria gone already?

"Jennifer," he says.

She waits. Then she rolls the caster-footed chair forward, sits before her impressive stacks of hard copy, and waits some more.

"Look. Jennifer, something went wrong with my upbringing. The only time I'm fluent is when I'm smashed, and then I turn into the maddened wolfman. So I don't go out very often. For example. Six months ago, after a horrible divorce, I ventured to a party without a keeper. Nobody tied me up or shoved a gag in my face. I failed conspicuously to recognize an old acquaintance, and then hectored him about the polarity of his sexual cravings. In the crudest possible terms. With no provocation, I noisily engaged a stern feminist on the matter of her tits, which I found noteworthy. I ended by shouting in a proprietorial manner from one end of the host's house to the other, at three in the morning, inviting young bearded people and their companions to drink up and depart swiftly, in what seemed to me a hearty and engaging fashion. When I got home I fell down in my own puke."

After a further silence, Jennifer lights a cigarette. "How horrible."

"Doubtless I'm a horrible person in every respect."

"That's not what I meant."

Rostow starts to yell, then lowers his voice in confusion. "I stumble over you sprawled on a fat bean-bag in the middle of a room of colleagues and strangers having your tits massaged by a swarthy blackamoor—"

She's on her feet. "Okay, sport. Enough. Out." Eddie is taken aback at the power of her extended arm as she hoists him off the desk. He thumps down heavily, barring the door with one leg.

"No, goddamn it. So I sit down beside you and toy with your wonderfully hairy leg. You smile and extend your limbs.

I can't believe it. Up goes my little hand, hoppity-scamp—"

"Shut up, you creep."

For this, Rostow is utterly unprepared. He gapes.

Jennifer refuses to lower her eyes. Blotches of color stand out on her cheekbones. "You're right, Rostow, you are a horrible person. Incredibly enough, I once found you rather piquant. Your crass behavior the other night might have been forgivable as whimsy." In authentic rage she clamps her teeth together and wrenches the door open. "Stay or go as you please." Then the room is vacant, and Rostow slumps on the desk with his guts spilling out of his wounds and his brain whirling into sawdust and aloes.

The bloody aura is a jolt from one awful dream to another. With iron control he keeps hold of the rabbit and wrenches his head around as vision clears. Three minutes after four. Yet the appalling encounter echoes like a double image, a triple image in fact. His chemistry overloads and he vomits uncontrollably. Finally sourness sweeps away hallucination; he totters to the console and runs the mirror system down to Latent.

Aghast, he tells himself: "Scrub it out. Make it didn't happen." Regressing to childhood. His mouth tastes repulsive; he wipes his lips on the back of his hand. I can't take much more of this, he thinks. The human frame wasn't meant to handle the strain of dual sets of information. It'd take a Zen roshi to cope with this weirdness. The bitch, the lousy bitch.

But it isn't Jennifer Barton's doing. Rostow is doomed by his oafishness. I've got to keep away from her. I'd shred myself into a million messy bits. It is clear, though, that he cannot cower forever in the lab with only a canonized rabbit for company. Enough, he tells himself. Out. The clock shows a quarter after four. Cyclic time is slipping away. Down the corridor, unharassed, Jennifer Barton is presumably finalizing her coiffure.

Rostow slams the door, running for the stairs. As he expects, Buonacelli and his claque are milling in the Senior Faculty Bar. Donaldson dispenses whiskies in their midst, jovial, exonerated, cautioning them all to reticence under the rubric of security.

"A wonderful experience, Dr., uh, Rostow?" says one of the directors, a pleasant administrator. Eddie turns convulsively. "I'm Harrison Macintyre, Ford Foundation." The man holds out his hand. "No problems with funding," he smiles, "after today."

"Oh. Thank you. Not 'doctor,' I'm afraid. I've never had time to write anything up." Stan seems to be explaining how the advanced-wave project sprang fully armed from his professorial brow. Adrenalin begins a fresh surge.

Macintyre puts liquor into his hand and asks, "I've been wondering about that. Publication, I mean. Surely today wasn't your first trial with the equipment?"

"No. No, Harrison. Call me Eddie. We knew it was going to work. It's been operational for some weeks." Across the russet carpet, Buonacelli is laughing boomingly. "The Nobel Prize for Physics, Stan," says the senator. "The Nobel Prize for Medicine," adds a beaming director. "Hot damn," cries another "they'll make it a hat trick and give you the Nobel Prize for Literature when your paper comes out."

Rostow scowls hideously. "Normally we would indeed have published by now, Harrison," he says loudly. "But after the tachyon fiasco, Professor Donaldson developed some misgivings about shooting his mouth off prematurely, you see." Faces turn. "You must remember. Every man and his dog was hunting faster-than-light particles. The great physicist spied his chance at glory." The Ford Foundation man, scandalized, tries to hush him. Eddie drains his glass, gestures for another. "But the professor blew it. His tachyons were actually pickup calls from the Green Cab Company. They snuck in through his Faraday cage. Someone didn't check that out until after the press conference did we, Stan?"

Donaldson is peering at the half-full glass in Rostow's grasp; slowly, he allows his gaze to rise until he studies a point somewhere near Eddie's left ear. "Mr. Rostow," he says from the depths of his soul, "hired hands are rarely invited into this room. Those who gain that privilege generally comport themselves with civility and a due measure of deference. Those who have just been fired without a reference do not linger here under any circumstances. Get out of my sight."

Jennifer Barton arrives at that moment, smiling, hair lustrous. At the door she hesitates, scanning shocked faces. Their eyes meet. Her presence—oblivious of edited outrage, witness to new humiliation—sends Rostow into a frenzy. He throws down his glass and catches Donaldson by his lapels.

"I wish you wouldn't shout, Frog-face," he says, every sinew on fire. "You astounding hypocrite," he says, jouncing the man back on his heels. "What's a Nobel Prize or two between hired hands?" he says, thumping Donaldson heavily in the breast. Two or three of the directors have come to their senses by now and grapple with Rostow, dragging him away from his gasping and empurpled victim. "It happens all the time, doesn't it?" Eddie squirms, kicking at targets of opportunity. "We poor bastards break our asses so some ludicrous discredited figurehead can whiz off to Stockholm to meet the king."

Even in his own ears, Rostow's outburst sounds thin, thin. Where righteousness should ring, only a stale peevishness lingers. Tears of anger and mortification star the pendant cut-glass lamps. He breaks free and pushes through business suits. Jennifer stares at him, off balance. "You don't want to stay with these vultures," he cries, seizing her arm. It seems that she studies his scarlet face for minutes of silence. With a minimal movement she dislodges his hand.

"Eddie," she says regretfully, "when are you going to grow up?"

Bitch. Bitch, bitch.

And the bloody aura. He is holding the rabbit, wrenching his head around to check the clock. This time the shock of recurrence is curiously attenuated, as if lunatic hostility sits better than misery with a physiology keyed to fright. Rostow's heart rattles, catches its beat; the pulse thunders in his neck and wrists. The rabbit struggles free. He moves with Tarquin's ravishing stride to the console, at a pitch of emotion. Icily he shuts down the mirror system. There are cracks in the concrete where the supports for the magnetic coils are embedded. A faint regular buzzing comes from the fluoros. His skin is crawling, as if each hair on his body is a nipple, erect and preternaturally sensitive. Gagging, he closes the door and paces remorselessly down the corridor.

Jennifer Barton stands on the bottom step of the carved stairs, deflecting Senator Buonacelli's horseplay. Rostow storms past them. "Hey, boy, that was a great show," cries the senator. "Why don't you and this little lady come up and join us in a drink?" Rostow hardly hears the man. His feet are at the ends of his legs. Jennifer's door is not locked. He leaves it wide for her. Staring out into the afternoon light. Three tall blacks fake and run, dribbling a ball.

"Well, Jambo!" As Eddie faces her, Jennifer is closing the door, meeting him with an infectious smile. "It's taken you long enough to find my office, sailor."

"What?" he says, uncomprehending. He pushes her roughly back against the crowded desk and takes her thigh with cruel pressure. Speechless and instantly afraid, she repudiates his hand. He thrusts it higher and tugs at her underwear.

"Let's pick up where we left off," he informs her. An absolute chill pervades his flesh. Nothing had prepared him to expect this of himself. Everything he calls himself is outraged, shrunken in loathing at his own actions.

"Stop it," she says distantly. "You fucking asshole." Tactically her posture is not favorable; when she drives up her right knee, its bruising force is deflected from his leg. I can have whatever I want. The whole universe is a scourge slashing at my vulnerable back. Very well, let those be the rules. He imagines he is laughing. I have nothing to offer but fear itself. As she begins to scream and batter his neck, his cheek, his temple, he clouts her savagely into semi consciousness. Oh Jesus, you can't be blamed for what happens during a nightmare. In the absence of causality, Fyodor, all things are permitted. She is bent backward, moving feebly. One of his hands clamps her mouth, hard against her teeth, the other unzips. I'm the Primary Process Man, oh, wow. But he is so cold. There is no blood under his skin. Rostow batters at her thighs with his limp flesh. He slides to his knees. The edge of the desk furrows his nose.

"You," Jenny grunts. She is blank with detestation. Tenderly, she touches her skull. "You."

Eddie Rostow lurches upright. Swaying, exposed, he falls into the corridor. The same young student, returning, regards him with astonishment and abhorrence. The boy reaches out a hand, changes his mind and pelts away in search of aid. It is all a grainy picture show, a world-sized monitor screen. They'll fire him for this. Oh, shit, Jenny, you don't understand, I *love* you.

In fugue, Rostow pitches down the corridor.

The cleaver is lying where Donaldson left it on the bench, a ripple of bunny blood standing back from its surgical edge. Rostow's self-contempt has no bounds. As he lifts the blade, there is one final lucid thought. I'm an animal, he tells himself. We can't be trusted. The cleaver's handle slips in his sweating fingers. He tightens his grip and with a kind of concentration brings the thing in a whirling silvery arc into the tilted column of his neck. Shearing through the heavy sterno-mastoid muscle, in one blow it slashes the carotid artery, the internal jugular and the vagus nerve, before it's stopped by the banded cartilage of the trachea. He scarcely feels his flesh open: all pain is in the intolerable impact. A brilliant crimson jet spears and spatters, but Rostow fails to see it: he collapses in shock, and the fluid pulses out of his torpid body until he is dead.

His corpse lies cooling until half a minute after 4:37.

A dizzying aura of bloody light spangled with pinpoints of imploding radiance momentarily blinds him.

Rostow screams.

There is nothing banal in this plunge upward into instantaneous rebirth. It is overwhelming. It is transcendental. It is a jack-hammer on Rostow's soul.

Like a thousand micrograms of White Lightning, life deto-nates every cell of his brain and body. He has been to hell, and died afterwards. Let me stay dead. Let me be dead.

Catharsis purges him of every thought. Eddie cradles the white rabbit in his arms and sobs his heart out.

At length he is sufficiently composed to reflect: I never cried when Tania left. Everything wise within me insisted that I should cry, but I turned my back. He realizes that he hasn't wept freely since he was a child. Dear Jesus, does it take this abomination to lance my constricted soul?

And his spirits do indeed soar. Without denying the reality of what he has done, his pettiness and spite and ignominy, he encompasses a mood of redemptive benediction. It brings a wide, silly grin to his mouth.

"Bunny rabbit," he declares, lofting the animal high over his head, laughing as its big grubby hind feet thump the air, "ain't nobody been where we wuz, baby. Let me tell you, buster, I like this side a lot better."

Eddie feeds the rabbit a strip of lettuce and steps through the tedious details of shutdown. He meditates on his humbling and his bestiality, flinching at memory.

The frailty at his core yearns to interpret it all as a stress nightmare, an hallucination. Denial would be not merely futile and cowardly, it would betray what has been offered him. Rather piquant, eh? Holy shit. Still, it is a point of access. Eddie Rostow confesses to his worst self that he needs all the help he can get.

The next cycle brings swifter recovery. Rostow splashes tepid water from the flask into his face, dabbing at his reddened eyelids. Soon he must spend some time figuring how to replicate the loop condition after he gets off this one. Fertile conjectures multiply; he suppresses them for the moment. Nerving himself, he walks edgily to the Software Center, nodding companion-ably to the passing student. The directors have ascended to their solace. His knock is tentative.

Jennifer's smile startles him with its warmth. She lowers her hairbrush. "Well, hello, sailor."

Eddie stands in the doorway, drinking her unbruised face. Despite himself he flushes.

"Don't just loiter there with intent, man. You're the unsung hero of the moment. It was sensational." She frowns. "I hated it with the rabbit, though."

"Jennifer," he says in a rush, "I'm sorry about the party. You know."

"That. Yeah. You were rather blunt."

"You inspire the village idiot in me."

"Sailor, that's the sweetest thing anyone ever. Coming up to poach on the Professorial Entertainment Allowance Fund?"

Eddie melts disgustingly within, wallowing in amnesty. "I happen to know a place."

"You've got a fifth of Jack Daniels squirreled in your locker."

"I've always admired your mind. Passionately."

"That wasn't the part you molested in public."

"I am, " he tells her, "truly sorry." Her hair flows in his fingers and he puts his face against hers for a moment. Jenny touches his hand.

"While we dally," she tells him, "Stan is up there screwing you,"

"No argument. He's like that. All scientists are lunatics and swindlers. I intend to fight. More to the point, are you screwing Dr. Singh? Oh Christ, don't answer that."

"I will not, it's none of your business. For God's sake, don't get snotty. Here, let me help you off with your—"

"Shouldn't we shut the door?"

"Kick it, you're closer. Why did it take you so long to get here?"

"Don't ask."

"Hmm. You know, I thought you were going to throw a tantrum in the lab."

Eddie tries to keep his tone light. "Upon my soul, Miss Barton, that'd be no way for a besotted genius to contest his rights." Shortly he asks: "Won't the printouts get runkled?"

"There's more in the computer, you fool."

On the next loop, abandoning his dazed inertia for an instant, Eddie glances at Jennifer's wrist watch and ensures that the flash comes as the flash comes as the flash comes

WALLS OF FLESH, BARS OF BONE

WITH BARBARA LAMAR

The question of whether the waves are something "real" or a function to describe and predict phenomena in a convenient way is a matter of taste. I personally like to regard a probability wave, even in 3N-dimensional space, as a real thing, certainly as more than a tool for mathematical calculations.... Quite generally, how could we rely on probability predictions if by this notion we do not refer to something real and objective?

Max Born, *Natural Philosophy of Cause and Chance*

Hanging onto the desk's edge, I eased myself back, then slumped down again while the floor got itself on an even keel. I'd drooled on the interdisciplinary dissertation I was meant to be assessing. Psychoanalytic cinema theory, always such fun these post-postmodern days. *Ob(Stet)Rick's: A/OB[GYN]jection, Blood and Blocked de(Sire) in CASA[BLANK]A.* I closed my eyes again, feeling ill.

Lissa was shocked. I wasn't all that pleased myself. Slightly reproachful, she said, "Dr. Watson, your appointment with the committee chair." I squinted at the blur of my watch, did a sweep of the cluttered surface of my desk. No glasses in immediate view. You need to be wearing them in order to see where they are, but if you're wearing them you already know where they are. That was the kind of pseudo-paradox this grad student's dissertation was cluttered with. The inside of my head gonged.

"Yeah." I tried to clear my throat. "Thanks, Liss."

"Ten minutes. Shall I bring you a cup of coffee?" Delivering coffee was explicitly not part of Lissa's job description as administrative assistant, but I seemed to bring out the motherly instinct in her, although she is too young by a generation and a half to be my mother.

"Sure. You're a sweetheart." Inside my head a Hell's Angels convention was thrashing their hogs and tearing the town apart. Probably shouldn't have brought that bottle of Jack Daniels to the office. Only meant to take a swallow to calm my nerves.

I shoved the (th)esis on to the floor, where it landed with a (th)ud, then dug through the random drifts of paperwork on my desk. My reading glasses were three layers down. I jammed them on my face. Where the hell had I put the notes for the meeting? I was stern: Lee, my boy, do this in an orderly manner. Here was the title page from Jerry Lehman's chapter on the effects of adrenergic stimulants on the signification behavior of non-autistic children. I was supposed to be reviewing the damned thing. Two months behind so far but I'd catch up, soon as I got things worked out with Beverley.

Map of Vancouver. Another unfinished dissertation I was supposed to be supervising: *Queer Lear, Queen*. Brochure advertising whole-house entertainment systems. Article from the *Irish Journal of Post-Psychoanalytic Semiotics* I'd been meaning to read.

"Here you go, Dr. Watson. Fresh from the microwave." Lissa set the cup down on a small bare spot on the credenza behind me. Even before I took the first sip I could tell it was stale, left over from 7:30 in the morning. What the hell, this was medicine.

"Can I help you look?" She glanced at her watch; her voice held a tinge of panic. Funny, I wasn't a bit tense, and it was my career that was on the line. Up for promotion to associate professorship, financial security and independence for the rest of my life. Fat chance.

"I'm looking for the notes I need for the meeting with Patterson. It would be six pages stapled together."

"Handwritten?" Good girl. Woman. Person. She was already attacking the mounds of papers.

"Printed." I leaned back in the leather chair Bev had given me three, no, five years ago, sipping my awful coffee. All the time in the world. I'll be okay, I told myself. I'll be fine, soon's the caffeine takes hold.

"I can't find them anywhere, Dr. Watson." Lissa pushed her hair back from her forehead, sighed. "Are you sure you brought them to the office?"

I goggled my eyes sadly behind my goggles and shook my head. I wasn't sure of anything these days, except that if I let myself think too hard it hurt too much. "It's okay, Lissa. I can wing it." I stood up and the floor was steadier. "Better get going."

"Like that?"

I glanced down at my Dept. Of Psychoceramics tee shirt with a pang. A gift from daughter Mandy the year before the dreaded menarche hormones kicked in and she went from adorable to teen werewolf. Lissa was right. It was a little frayed around the edges, and maybe the sentiment wasn't ideal for the inquisition. "Not to worry." I kept a suit jacket hanging behind the door for emergencies. Buttoned up snug, started out, stepping lively, a man who knows where he's going and what he's doing. But when I got out to the hall, away from the safety of my own office, I stopped short. Professor H. Patterson would expect me to say something at least moderately intelligent. You didn't get to be a committee boss in the Department of Psychosemiosis and Literature at the University of California at Davis without expectations of that sort. And I realized I didn't have anything remotely clever to tell her and the committee. Furthermore, I didn't give a shit. There was a probability of about 0.5 that canceling the meeting now would end my career. On the other hand, if I went in there half crocked...oh c'mon Watson, not half, 80% at least...truthfully, the probability was close to 1.0 that I'd be out on my ass with no further ado, and so much for tenure, increasingly a dead letter. What the hell.

"Lissa?" I looked over my shoulder, tried for my most pleading, boyish look. "Do me a favor?"

"Call Professor Patterson and tell her you've had a stroke."

"Something like that, yeah. Um...." Mental wheels turned sluggishly. "Tell her they called from my daughter's school and there's been a crisis and I had to go right away." Like anyone would call me about anything connected with my child.

"I didn't know you and Bev had kids."

"One. Not Bev's, from a former...marriage."

"You're a dark horse, Dr. Watson."

I grabbed my helmet and cantered off for the Department's outer door as fast as I could without tripping over any of my legs, and en passant grabbed a square, flat package from my inbox. No return address. Another orphan film from my mysterious benefactor, had to be. My spirits lifted as I made my escape to a brilliant afternoon that smelled of sage and ripe crabapples.

§

My apartment was dark and empty, though, shades drawn against the afternoon light, as it had been for the five months I sulked in it. My estranged wife Beverley used to find me pathologically optimistic, but that was before she threw me out. I could picture the mocking way she'd raise her eyebrows at me if she could see how eagerly I opened the mailbox and scanned the bills and junk mail for her handwriting. No such luck; instead, there was a letter from Virta and Crump, P.C., Bev's lawyers. I tossed it on the deal-with-it-later pile along with a couple of month's worth of bills and headed for the fridge. Nothing like a cold beer to take the edge off incipient depression.

The package was indeed an orphan film. The label on the slightly rusty metal canister read "#11: Reverend Willard D. Havard, New York City, January 10, 1931." No accompanying letter or card. Now that I was living on my own, the movie screen and the old Bell & Howell Filmosound projector had become a regular feature of the décor, so there was no need to set up. I took a swig of beer and began threading the film through the machine.

Orphan films are movies that have been abandoned by their owners, sometimes because of copyright problems, more often because they didn't seem worth saving. But films that seemed worthless soon after they were made—old newsreels, for example—are now priceless windows into the past. I'm easily entertained and can spend hours absorbed in some unknown family's home movies from the 1950s. Whoever was sending these mystery films seemed to be a connoisseur with finer tastes than mine. He or she was sending stuff from the earliest days of simultaneously recorded picture and sound.

Film #11 was only a little over 3 minutes long. At the beginning, a tall bearded man with a Santa Claus belly was delivering a sermon on a street corner. The sound was scratchy, and you could hear car engines and horns honking in the background, but still you could make out most of the Reverend's pitch.

"On my way down here today, I saw a little girl, couldn't of been more than five or six. This little child was standing on the sidewalk selling chewing gum and mints. I asked myself, brothers and sisters, why is this little girl standing here selling chewing gum instead of sitting at a desk at school? Is she just trying to get some spending money? Is she helping to support her family?"

He had a certain charisma. It took an effort to redirect my attention from the Rev. Willard to his audience, if you could call eight or ten motley hobo types plus a couple of young boys an audience. One of the kids gave the other a rough shove as I watched; this was returned with compound interest, and soon they were rolling on the sidewalk like a couple of tomcats.

The Reverend reached the climax of his presentation. "As I was telling you earlier my friends, God sends us trials and tribulations to give us a chance to shine in His Light."

A fellow about my age had passed in front of him, turned his head quickly to the camera and then away. Startled, I blinked, but he was gone. The scuffling boys seemed so intent on their struggle that they'd lost track of where they were. One landed with a thud on an ancient duffle bag. Its elderly owner thwacked both the kids across the shoulders with his cane. Indignant, for a moment they stopped fighting, then the sound track of the film clearly picked up the shorter kid yelling at the taller one, "Your mother's a [something] slut." And they were rolling on the ground again, just as the Reverend Willard reached for his tambourine, which had been passed from hand to hand. The full weight of both boys slammed against the Reverend's shins; he went down on his massive butt, the tambourine went flying, scattering a few coins across the sidewalk. Instantly the boys stopped their scuffling. The taller kid, closer to the lens, grabbed a couple of coins. The other, grinning, ducked down so his face was visible under an armpit, and did something that flashed white and was gone. Instantly, then, both boys ran swiftly and gleefully out of the frame, their differences apparently forgotten. And that was it. The end of the film.

I rewound a short way and played the last few seconds again. There had been something familiar about that fellow walking past, something that prickled the back of my neck.

No mistaking it, once noticed and reviewed. It gave me the strangest shiver. I watched that segment of the film again, and again, and once more again. He was me. I mean, the guy bore an uncanny resemblance to yours truly. Allowance made for the antique style of his clothing and his cap, the very spittin' image. That was undeniably me in the 1931 movie. The year before my grandmother was born.

I saw something else that creeped the hell out of me: just before the scuffling lads rammed into the Reverend Santa Claus, my double turned his head, caught the eye of the photographer, and winked at him. In effect, through the recording lens, at me.

What the fuck?

My hangover was gone, and my lethargy. Adrenalin can do that. I wanted to look more closely at this fragment of images from the past without risking the fragile orphan footage any further. It took me an hour setting up the old mirror box that reflects the image from screen to camcorder lens (I'd bought it on eBay, they don't make them any more), and then saved the digital feed to my hard drive. Doing this properly would require a bunch of money and a professional transfer house tech, lifting off the dust and other crap from eighty years of careless storage, paying frame by frame attention to brightness and other parameters. Maybe I'd get to that, but my grant money for orphan restoration had just about run dry, and I wanted something quick and fairly easy.

I opened the vid and went straight to the appearance of the guy who looked like me. And the kids, horsing around. I ran it twice, then went to the kitchen cabinet and opened another bottle of Jack Daniels.

"Your mother's a toboggan-time slut," the smaller kid had yelled, or something like that. And then he reached into his raggedy gray shirt and pulled out a sheet of glistening white paper, except that it looked more like an impossibly thin, flexible iPad, held it up for just thirty frames, jammed the thing back under cover again, and they were away.

The iPad that wasn't an iPad held several...what? Hieroglyphs? No, mostly Roman and Greek letters, upper and lower case, with some other items that might have been Arabic or for all I knew Assyrian. And a few numerals, subscripts and superscripts, and brackets. Equations, okay. The only equations I'm familiar with are the bogus propositions of Jacques Lacan, psychiatrist and Freud-fraud. I did a screen capture of the clearest frame, pushed it up to 400%. Blurry, but I felt sure a mathematician would have no trouble recognizing it. Or a physicist, or cosmologist, or the creature from Bulgaria, whatever.

The trouble with Google is that you can't easily search for equations, or at least I couldn't. I tried to cut and paste the bit-mapped string of symbols and that didn't get me anywhere. I went laboriously into Word, found the symbols one by one, but half of those on the screen were unknown to Microsoft, far as I could tell. I plugged in the fragment of the single equation whose parts I could find and hit "I'm Feeling Lucky."

This first and simplest equation popped onto the monitor, embedded in an only moderately incomprehensible paper on a site called arXiv, which I assumed was an archive for people from the Other Culture who couldn't spell, like Bev's current creature.

$$|\psi> = \Sigma\ (a_i\ \exp(j\varphi_i)\ |\ x_i, y_i, z_i, v_i, \omega_i >)$$

It was dated 2009. The paper was titled "Ordinary Analogues for Quantum Mechanics," by one Arjen Dijksman, and it began: "Upon pondering over the question 'What is ultimately possible in physics?', various interrogations emerge. How could one interpret ultimately? Is there an ultimatum, a final statement in physics, after which one could say 'Physics is finished'? Are there issues, for instance fundamental principles, beyond which we could not go past? How can we describe the boundary between the possible and the impossible in physics? Anyway, does such a boundary exist? And if so what is at the edge?"

I ran the whole video file again, and this time the Jack Daniels didn't keep me warm. The kid hadn't shouted "toboggan." My skin crawled. Jesus Christ. He'd said "teabaggin'." And the emphasis was subtle, but it wasn't "teabaggin'-time slut." It was "teabaggin' time-slut."

Teabaggers in 1931? Give me strength. Had they even invented teabags that long ago? Back to Google, fingers stiff and clumsy on the keys. Yes, a form of silk tea- bag was used as early as 1903, but today's rectangular teabag came along as late as 1944. Let's not be too literal, Lee, let's try a lexical search.

Before the current burst of radical crazies calling themselves the Tea Party, mocked by their foes as "teabaggers," the term had another and more scabrous sense. Urban Dictionary told me "teabagging" meant "To have a man insert his scrotum into another person's mouth in the fashion of a teabag into a mug with an up/down (in/out) motion." I squeezed my eyes shut. Oh-kay. Whatever floats your boat. But that had to be a recent coinage, didn't it, post-1944 at least? Maybe not. Old slang from society's undergrowth tends to seep up again and again, then vanish for a time. But "time-slut." And the arXiv abstract. Urchins didn't know about quantum theory in 1931. Maybe nobody did. I felt my ignorance yawning at me.

I was in a sort of numb dissociated state, trying to remain amused at this obvious Photoshopped fake someone had shoved in my pigeon hole to mess with my peace of mind, but increasingly angry at whoever treated me with such scorn. Even if, face it, I was a barely controlled drunk two or three steps away from the same skids as those bums in the 1931 movie.

But that was the point, it wasn't a 1931 movie, of course, it was a bricolaged fake. Well, maybe not the whole thing. Mostly it looked highly authentic to my well-seasoned eye. They'd rendered my face into the image of the young man, and somehow worked in that iPad thing for a few frames. Maybe in the original the kid had waved a newspaper headline, or a cloth cap. So why the hell bother? Who was trying to tell me something, and what? A disgruntled student? A post-postmodern gag to piss me off, get my goat? One of Bev's sardonic tame "artists"?

I shut the machine down, carefully backing everything up first to the university cloud, and biked over to the other side of town to see Bev. Virta and Crump and impending divorce be damned. I just couldn't cope with this shit by myself, and besides I was developing a suspicion or two.

§

When I first met Bev Peacock during my guest lectures at Chicago's School of the Art Institute, her father owned a small chain of health food stores with corporate headquarters in Sacramento. Bev took a couple of summer courses at UC Davis, including my sessions on Julia Kristeva and other psychoanalytic deep thinkers on their way to superannuation. During her last two years in Chicago, emails fled between us; we talked on the phone at least twice a day. By then, I was separated from Sheila, and visited Chicago when I could, strolling with Bev in Lincoln Park, visiting the art museum where I spent more time looking at her than at the daubings. Everyone could see we were in love, for the first two years, anyway. As I sank ever deeper into gloom at the gibberish I was required to teach, Bev discarded her dreams of great art. The renunciation changed her, bit by bit; she built her separate life, embarrassed to be seen with me: my moods, my drinking, the way I dressed.

Barry Peacock sold the health food store chain six months after Bev and I married, netting $6.2 million. Barry and Ruth wanted their daughter to enjoy at least part of her inheritance while they were still around, so they bought the house in Davis for a little over a million dollars. The house remains owned by the Beverly Peacock Watson Separate Property Trust, but I had no claim to it under California's community property law. And now I was doubly alienated: evicted, replaced by the atom-tweaker from Bulgaria.

§

I leaned my Koga StreetLiner against a pillar of the porch and dropped my helmet into the saddlebag. I felt queasy about leaving the Koga unlocked, even in this neighborhood, but one of the reasons Bev threw me out was my habit of parking bicycles in the house. The creature opened the door and gazed down at me benignly. He drew in a deep, energizing breath, then wrinkled his patrician nostrils at the eau d'Jack.

"Lee. I see the flesh seems a little weak today, but the spirit smells strong."

I winced. I hadn't drunk that much, although I'd weaved a little on my ride; it was probably just as well no cop had pulled me over to check my sang froid. My sang réal. I sniggered. "And how's your cat today, Schrödinger? Alive or dead?"

Tsvetan Toshtenov, D.Sc. (Ruse) blocked the doorway. "Both, actually. As a matter of fact, we've just done a...." He shook his head. "Of course you don't want to know. What do you want, Lee? I assumed Bev had a restraining order."

"Ha ha, very droll." I made myself small and went under his arm, then galumphed down the hallway . Two small boys glanced up from their Playstation 4 and gazed at me impassively. So now she'd moved in the entire family. Those faces. Something went ping in a buried part of my brain but I was too aerated to catch it even though I half-stumbled for an instant. It would come back to me. I jinked through our bright metal-clad kitchen warm with the odors of Bulgarian fare, and made for the studio out back. "Honey, I'm ho-o-o-ome," I yodeled.

It wasn't a studio, of course, despite the artfully placed and prepped canvas on its easel awaiting the first lick of oil. It had been waiting for years. When I'd married Beverley and moved in here with her, she was in the last drawn-out ebbings of her passion to be a painter, heading step by inexorable step toward curatorship and a safe doctorate in Mapplethorpe and de Kooning (Elaine, naturally, not Willem). These days she organized elegant or bizarre installations, events, displays, online video performances. If anyone was likely to know a scamp capable of torturing me with a fake orphan movie, at her instigation, it was Bev. She of all people knew my own passion for orphan footage. Yet it seemed a bit beneath her, and perhaps beyond Bev's currently limited quotient of whimsy.

"Drunk! For heaven's sake, Lee." My wife rose from her persuasive replica something[th]-century oak Chateau Something credenza and advanced in her forceful and menacing way toward me. "What are you doing here?"

"Hardly drunk," I said without conviction. "The sun's well and truly over the yardarm, Bev."

"I had a call from Hattie Patterson several hours ago. She wondered if I knew where you'd got to."

"Why would she expect you to know?"

"We are still married, Lee. Have you signed the documents yet? Hattie said you didn't show up at the faculty meeting convened to consider your candidacy, and it had something to do with your daughter. Is Mandy okay? Oh, wait, of course she is—I should have taken it for granted you were lying."

The spring, such as it was, had quite left my step. I looked for somewhere to sit, and found a deck chair rather ruined by splashes of house paint leaning against one wall. As I started to open it, Bev gave a strangled cry.

"Not that, you idiot. Good god, man, it's an early Rauschenberg."

I backed away smartly. So it was, or could be. How the hell did Beverley get her hands on something like that? She was loaded, but not that loaded, or Virta and Crump, P.C. were lying through their teeth. Of course that was the specialty of divorce attorneys. Or maybe she'd brought it home from some exhibition for a couple of weeks of private gloating. I opened my mouth to ask, an instant too late.

"Come on, inside the house with you, and then please leave. I don't want the children to see a drunkard shambling about." She shepherded me out of the studio and along the small vegetable garden and ample green lawn where we had once rolled naked. Her creature was waiting in the kitchen, coffee mug in hand. He passed it to me and I burned my mouth.

"That place is the death of the soul, Bev," I told her. "You know that much yourself. I mean, it's not as if you stayed around to build your academic...." I trailed off, blowing across the top of the mug. A teabagging time-slut? I couldn't imagine Bev and the creature from Bulgaria engaging in reckless sports of that kind. Not that she and I hadn't enjoyed, when we were first together, our share of—

The two little boys crouched in the next room noisily killing aliens and cavorting in three-dimensional havoc with imaginary super-weapons were not her children, not ours, but Tsvetan's, and nobody of my acquaintance had ever seen their mother, save the creature himself. Beverley had met him at a soiree of daubers and their hangers-on. He'd pronounced himself a cubist. No doubt Bev raised an eyebrow. Hardly au courant. No, no. Forgiving urbane laughter over a simple error. A QBist. A

Quantum Bayesian. Whatever that was, I'd never bothered to ask. As for his prior woman, the mother of his brats, maybe she was a time-slut. Whatever that might be. After all, how else— Ridiculous, I told myself, slurping and blowing. I'm delusional. This is worse than the DTs. Those kids can't be older than five and seven. I couldn't remember their names. Something eastern European. Ivaylo and Krastio? But the little one did look horribly familiar. I could all too easily imagine him whipping out an advanced display unit from under his shirt. In five or six years from now. Christ.

"I'm sure you'd like a drink," the creature said, and handed me a large glass not quite brimming with a deep, rich pinot noir. I remembered those glasses; they'd been a wedding gift from my aunt Hilda. I considered quaffing it in one hit and then flinging it into the fireplace, but that doesn't really work with a top of the line gas cooking range. I sipped in a gentlemanly manner, sat at the new kitchen table, and told them in a not especially accusatory tone about the Rev. Willard D. Havard and his unusual sidewalk congregation.

"You can access this video, presumably?"

"If I'd brought my laptop with me, Bev, I'd be delighted to show it to you."

The creature was gone; he was back almost instantly with a gleaming titanium-shelled Apple. He pushed it in front of me. The university log-in box was displayed.

"Oh hell, why not?" I pulled my orphan out of the cloud and ran it as they stood behind me, watching with a blend of avidity (Tzvetan) and amusing contempt (my faithless wife). At the end of the three minutes I said, "Again?" and reran it. Then I found the screen capture and blew it up on the rather nice large display.

"Well. That's obviously ket quantum notation. Dirac didn't invent it until 1939, so clearly this film isn't from 1931, did you say?"

"Sweetheart," Bev said in a strangled voice, "didn't you notice? Those were Wolf and Chris." I looked up; her face was totally pale, and her eyes were fixed on Sweetheart. "Those were your boys, grown up."

"Distant relatives, perhaps." Tsvetan was doubtful, but I trusted Bev's curatorial eye, and I imagine my own face was as bloodless as hers. "In 1939, my own parents and their siblings were still under Hitler's boot." Or working for the Gestapo, I didn't quite mutter aloud. I had no reason to think badly of the man's antecedents. For all I knew they had indeed been subjected to the banality of evil. "Show me that equation again, I thought I recognized it."

"I found it here." I opened the arXiv paper.

"I've heard of Arjen," the QBist said thoughtfully. "Young Dutch theorist with an interest in the foundations of physics, lives near Paris. He's a serious scholar, wouldn't have anything to do with a silly game like this, I assure you. Here, let me find his number." He had his iPhone out, with a finger sweeping.

"Please don't," I said. "I'm sure you're right. It's a prank by one of Bev's students."

My wife's jaw dropped. *"Excuse me?"*

"Who else has the skills to paste my head on some ancient young geezer's body, let alone do something to the appearance of the boys? Age shifting or whatever the forensic cops call it."

"Anyone over the age of ten," Bev said frostily. "Mandy, for that matter, or one of her friends. Have you been upsetting your daughter, Lee?"

"Oh for god's sake, I wasn't making it a personal accusation. My point was—"

"No, that's right, she's made it clear she doesn't want you in her life any longer. Sensible child."

I shoved the chair back with a nasty screeching sound. That wouldn't have helped the parquet floor. Tsvetan slipped into its seat like a large muscular eel and started pounding the keyboard. I noticed that he used only four fingers, but his typing was faster than I could manage with ten. Then again, scientists don't have to stop and think what they're about to be writing, it's all formulae and algorithms and canned knowledge, isn't it. Unless they're Einstein. Or Dirac, whoever he was. Dirac, I thought, sniggering silently to myself. Diracula.

"We're hungry." Two little boys with the same face as their father and no resemblance to Bev stood at the open door between the kitchen and the hall. They were amazingly well-behaved, nothing like the scapegraces they'd been in 1931. But it was them, they, I knew it, on the orphan footage. Had been. Would be. No question. Time was out of joint big time. I thought I was going to throw up.

"In a moment, darlings. This man was just leaving."

I shook my head sadly at the perfidy of women, children and creatures, swigged down the last of the red in my glass (my glass!), put the glass, stem first, in my jacket pocket, and walked in a dignified fashion to the front door, pursued by imprecations.

§

I warmed up some refried beans, which I suppose made them re-refried, and googled quantum theory, grinding my teeth from time to time. It was the sort of thing I'd have expected Carl Jung to get excited about, and of course he had been involved in a sterile collaboration with the physicist Wolfgang Pauli before Pauli came to his senses and decided synchronicity was a lot of hogwash. Bohr thought nothing was until it was observed, which might not have appealed to Freud, who thought all sort of unobserved items got up to no end of mischief. Granted, the way to eradicate and heal the mischief was to haul out the unobserved into the open, but then Bohr and Heisenberg (it said on my screen) insisted that you couldn't really get away with that, or only a bit at a time. I gave up, washed my plate, made some coffee, and called Mandy. That meant dealing with her mother first, but somehow I got through that ordeal and onto my sweet daughter.

"What do you want?"

"Don't you mean 'What the fuck do you want, Daddy dearest'? Don't answer that. Can't a man call his own—"

"I'm hanging up."

"Mandy, did you or one of your friends make that video of me? And the Toshtenov boys?"

In the background I heard someone incredibly famous and fatuous, someone observed at every moment of the day and night by hundreds of millions if not billions, of whom I knew nothing beyond their unlikely names. Beyoncé, or Lady Gaga, or Rihanna, or Bran'Nu. (I try. It makes my brain itch, but I do try. Fourteen year olds are feral.) Talk about quantum observers and ontological status. If anyone existed on the planet because of being observed, they were it. Talk about the evil of banality. After a long moment, my daughter said: "What?" Another silence. I waited. Then, with acid adolescent contempt: "Who would make a vid of you?"

"That's what I'm trying to find out, my good-natured offspring. Okay, look, I'll send you a tinyurl. The orphan's short."

"What?"

"Just let me know what you think. Okay? This is really important to me, Mandy."

"Whatever." She clicked off.

I fiddled about with my notes for the next day's lecture, thoughts skittering everywhere, and finally abandoned that as a really pointless exercise. Manfully, I kept away from the Jack Daniels. My daughter didn't call back or email me or text me or instant message me or tweet me, hardly to my surprise, but it was a bit disheartening. My Tivo was showing me a light, so I watched the ep of *Californication* it had grabbed while I wasn't paying attention ("Mr. Bad Example," which seemed somehow oracular), then had a shower, took a sleeping pill, and went to bed. At five in the morning I woke up with a headache and a woman standing in my dark bedroom. She said something.

"Hmngh?"

"She put it on the web."

I climbed out of bed naked, clawing for my trousers. The woman didn't shift her gaze from my face. "Who the hell are you and how did you get—"

"Went viral."

I clapped my hands and the bedside lamp came on. The woman was medium height, with a dark razor-brush 'do, and looked incontestably Bulgarian: long elegant nose, broad brow, widely spaced eyes. I had fancied to discern the creature in the immature features of the boys Wolf and Chris, but now I found the other half of the taller kid's genome, if not his half-brothers's. Good god, was the creature devoted to spreading his seed across the world? I said, "You'll be the time-slut, then."

She said, "Beg pardon?" All the women I'd met recently appeared to have formed a secret club dedicated to taking umbrage at everything I said to them. Except Lissa, I thought muzzily, and rubbed grit out of my eyes.

"I apologize, Mrs. Toshtenov. Having a hard time lately, not thinking all that clearly. Forgive me for being naked in my own bedroom."

"Is nothing haven't seen before."

"No doubt."

She clucked her tongue. "Radka. Not married. Am mother to Ivaylo."

I nodded. "Wolf."

"Means 'wolf,' yes."

"You sent me a message," I said, and finished getting dressed. "Then my bad-tempered daughter put it on YouTube, I take it. If that was your intention, why not just do it yourself? I thought it was fake, but now I—"

"Not much time," Radka told me. She bounced on her toes, almost vibrated with tension. "Listen. Am professor theoretical physics, Sofia. Not yet, soon. Listen, listen, keep mouth shut. Bohr wrong, of course. Bohm, wrong. Heisenberg not even wrong. QBists, half right." She went out like a light. I hadn't clapped my hands. A young woman in her early twenties stood several inches to the right of Radjka's last jitter. Her hair was cropped close, a sort of tie-dyed version of the Bulgarian fashion statement. I recognized her at once.

"Mandy," I yelped, and took a hesitant step, afraid to embrace her. The ghost of Christmas Future.

She stayed still, also vibrating. "Amanda. Hello, Dad. No, stay there. Everyone's observing this, see, that's the point. Everyone. Everything. Forever, probably. Well, near enough."

I sat down on the edge of the bed again and put my head in my hands. "I hope you're not going to tell me the Reverend Willard sent you."

"What?"

"Oh my god, are we back to that again?" I peeked through my fingers. Amanda sent me a wry grin.

"That was then. See, I do remember. Oh, I suppose it's now, too, if you look at it that—" She cleared her throat. "It's an entanglement excursion," Amanda told me. "Probability waves bouncing around an attractor, making the droplets walk, you know? We're just walls of flesh, Daddy, wrapped around bars of bone. And tangled."

A fragment of an old Bob Dylan song twanged in the back of my defeated skull. "Tangled up in blue." I let some words slip out, out of key but maybe that's how you have to sing Dylan: "All the people we used to know, they're an illusion to me now."

For a moment I thought my daughter was going to say "What?" again, but she caught herself and grinned again, more broadly this time. "Some are mathematicians," she said. It made me happy. Mandy the teen brat despised Dylan. "Tzvetan, for one. Go and talk to him."

"I thought he's a phys—" I started and she winked away. The creature of science stood in my bedroom, regarding me from a superior vantage. I couldn't quite keep my eyes on him. After-images flickered around the man. Christ, that's all I need, I told myself. Epilepsy. Or migraine, was it? Auras, battlements, fortification figures on the retina or, rather, deep inside the screwed-up brain. Jerry Lehman's chapter had something on the topic. I couldn't recall what. I'm so slack, I thought. And I used to be the boy wonder of psychoanalytic semiotics, back when that was the sexy thing to be a boy wonder in. "Can I help you,

Dr. Toshtenov? It's rather early, a mug of coffee? Heart starter? I was just talking to your...." Your what? I trailed off.

"Radka," he said. "Yes. No coffee. Sit down, Dr. Watson. I can't stay long, and we have a lot to cover." Tzvetan Toshtenov, with surprising levity (of a rather heavy-handed kind, I supposed, although I had no notion what it meant), wore a tee-shirt urging me to *Please adjust your priors before leaving the QBicle.* "What do you know about quantum entanglement and Bayesian probability theory?"

I gave him a sour look. "If we're going to play one-upmanship, Schrödinger, what do you know about, oh, the imbricated relationship between the Real, the Symbolic and the Imaginary?"

He looked at me suspiciously. "As in imaginary time? The teh dimension? Yes, that's relevant."

"As in the Lacanian orders of—Oh, never mind. Think of them as the three rings of a Borromean knot. That's three tangled rings that fall apart if one of them is cut. Like the middle rings in the Olympic symbol, but more so, or maybe not quite." I knew I was babbling, but I could see where that item of gibberish had popped up from: the entanglement Mandy mentioned. Future Amanda. And Bob Dylan.

"Chain. Borromean topological chain," the creature said, looking mildly astonished. "That's exceptionally astute, Watson, I didn't think you had it in you."

"No, it's a knot." He looked pained, as if once again I'd fallen in his estimation, and I quickly babbled: "Lacan argued that psychosis is what happens when the Borromean knot unravels, unless it's held in place by a fourth ring."

"A sinthome," Tzvetan the mathematician-physicist-smartass said. "Exactly. An extra link to the ring chain, a double curve. One ring to rule them all, as my boys would put it." He smiled fondly. "A bond through teh supertime. That's what holds the chain together. Holds everything. Do you see, Watson? Everything is nothing but uncertainties, latencies, probability pilot waves perhaps, vapors threaded in fog—until it is observed into definiteness and clarity."

"They teach you this stuff in Bulgaria, do they?"

He was gone. "Ha ha," I said weakly. "I unobserved you." I lay down and covered my eyes with one sweating forearm. Obviously I was ripe for the laughing academy. My Borromean chain had been pulled, and I was sliding down the cloaca maxima. I just wanted to go back to sleep, but when I made a feeble attempt to clap the light off there was already too much morning illumination coming in through the blinds. A voice said, from the center of the room, "Watson, come here, I need you." Bev's voice. Our old joke, and thank you, Alexander Graham Bell. She wasn't there. I put my socks and loafers on and started for the front door and my bike. Everything happened at once.

It wasn't the Rapture, and it wasn't the Cloud of Unknowing. This was the Cloud of Knowing Too Much, the silver lining of the dark night of the soul blazing like a thousand suns, like the Buddhist ten thousand things, the unity and diversity of everything bonded into its clasp, and I stood at the middle of it all but that was also at the edge, and at every point in between. Walls of flesh, bars of bone, gates of light, opening.

Mandy in my trembling arms, so tiny, so ugly, so incomprehensibly beautiful, eyes squeezed shut, head still slightly deformed by the terrible passage through her mother's body to this cold, brilliantly lit place. Sheila, holding up her arms for the baby, her own face shiny with sweat, exhausted, exultant. I bent to kiss her, Mandy cradled—An old lady with frosted hair and a look of synthetic peace on her harsh face, stretched in an open coffin. I bent and could not bring my lips to touch hers. The eyes of a hundred students locked to mine or skittering away or dully drooped to their laptops as I stood at the fulcrum of the lecture theater teasing them with text and context. "There is no outside-the-text," I said. "So we are told inside a text by Derrida: *Il n'y a pas de hors-texte.* So we carry that meaning outside, away from his text, reading it, observing it from as many angles as we can, remake it as our text, or discard it as waste, order into ordure, or vice versa, as supplement, so that it becomes, paradoxically—" With Beverley, young love redivivus, I stood, I stand, I will stand before paintings, etchings, constructs, texts that are all at once or seem to be, even as the eye skips and snacks and rebuilds, Picasso's wonderful African contortions, *Les Demoiselles d'Avignon*, his cubism, his late hideous, marvelous *Nude Woman with a Necklace*, and of course the once-fashionable distortions and visual paradoxa of Dali, Escher, Magritte, the decompressions into art that denied itself as art, Rauschenberg, Johns, Lichtenstein, the comic antics of Warhol and Koons and a thousand others, Dadists, Fauves, frauds, Freudians, unpeelers of pretense and its practitioners, and through it all the slowly ebbing passion, the curdling of my cynical eye observing everything into nothing.... All of this a millionfold, birth, copulation, and death.

"Bev," I said, "help me," and tears flooded down my face. I took a step and stood in the morning kitchen of our old house, our renovated house, the Edenic garden from which I'd exiled myself. Two little boys looked up from their bowls of cereal. Observing my manifestation from nowhere, the younger let out a piercing scream. The older yelled, "Tátko, that man has come back," and flung a spoonful of milk-soaked Rice Krispies at me, splashing my pants, like Luther hurling his ink bottle at the Devil. If it had been ink, a text in potentia, a zany part of my mind thought, it could have written a long bill of particulars, my crimes, every one. "Hush," I said. I held out my open, tear-wet hands. "Your daddy invited me here for breakfast, boys. Look, here he is now."

I am seated at the table, Bev's table, now his table. The boys have been driven to school. Tzvetan is saying, "I have to thank you most humbly, Dr. Watson. I couldn't have done it without your tip. And the boys, of course. But that's later." Nobody is in the room to look at us, but we are observed. The very air hums with the intensity of their gaze. Their gaze contributes, their gaze elicits, their gaze is the terrible look of a million million angels, more, vastly more, without judgment or pity, it seems to me. They do not act beyond the activity of their *Tat tvam asi*, their spectatorship. This is just the blather of my discipline, which I hardly credit any longer, but that is the function, obviously, of my own reciprocal gaze, and the mirror that is...well, the universe, the specular everything. And—

Appalling compression, emphatic dark clarity, in the infinitely protracted nothingness that awaits a first crystalline instant of precipitation. It is an eye in utter darkness. Something breaks, ruptures, breaches, raptures, bursts forth into its going and coming, fecund, a spray of light flung into the endless sphere of eyes gazing from within and without, making manifest, tumbling faster than light into categories that render themselves under that impossible gaze from the far ends of itself, from everywhere, forever. The sky foams with explosions boiling with a froth of stuff that swirls and settles and catches new light, a heaventree of galaxies, photonic dust etching their eidolons upon the eyes that watch and select and shape and build. My own eyes are there also, watching the lights redden and dissipate and fall away into night unendurably cold and empty. But that is the way of the thing, that is the story, all the eyes can do is witness until they are folded back into the great silence and void. Tzvetan is murmuring in my ear: "My experiment with single particle self-interference proved that a macroscopic extended object can be made to deviate through an instability threshold and surf its own pilot wave. But it can only do that because we chose to place it in that apparatus. We observe it from our own Bayesian priors, and its activity is objectively determined by the interaction between us and the particle. This is not mystical, Watson, stop curling your lip. It is the basis for everything that ever happens, to eternity and infinity."

I am aghast at the hubris. "So we're...engineering infinity?"

"No," he tells me, sharply. "Precisely not. We are nothing until we are observed by the universe. Infinity is engineering us."

Amanda handed me an old musty suit and a cloth cap. Of course I had seen them before. The world shimmered slightly, as if it were uncertain of itself. Two youngsters came into the studio—oh, that's where I was—dressed in Depression era knickerbockers suitable for urchins. The younger boy pushed a flat, flexible machine under his gray shirt, and winked at me.

"You're sending yourself a message, Lee," he said. "This is the moment we've all been waiting for."

I sent my daughter out of the room and dressed, dazed. "Who is going to send the orphan film to me?" I said.

"The universe," my ex-wife Bev told me at some time in the near future. She looked plumper, and a lot happier. Was she pregnant? Did the man pepper the planet with his offspring? "But I've found out who sent me that Rauschenberg, Lee, and I thank you. Of course, it will be a lot cheaper to buy it in 1951."

The universe looked at me, and I looked back, and found myself blinking in bright snowless winter afternoon light in New York, an older New York with far fewer of the great mirroring skyscrapers that will someday be built. Were. Up ahead, I saw the Reverend ranting, and I strolled past. Some nameless amateur cinematographer was cranking a Ciné-Kodak, and as I passed him I remembered the kid's cheeky wink and slipped the fellow one of my own. The two boys were horsing about, an irritated old geezer slapped out with his cane, but Krastio, the younger, had his eye focused on the middle distance. An intent, lovely woman in a long dowdy 1930s dress appeared out of nowhere at the entrance to a laneway. Quantum tunneled, I suppose Tzvetan would call it. Nobody but the younger boy and I saw her, except everyone and everything, forever. Krastio yelled out hoarsely to Ivaylo, "Your mother's at teh—begin time slot." He pulled out his display and flashed a page of equations to the rolling film. I walked briskly past, and took Radka's hand. The universe observed us in silence amid the rumbling noise of the city.

ALL MY YESTERDAYS

"My advice to you," said the psychiatrist, tapping his fingers on the polished top of his desk while he stared at the voluptuous Tiepolo on the far wall, "is a stiff dose of fornication."

The small man shook his head. "I'm sorry, but God won't allow it."

The psychiatrist injected a healthy trace of skepticism and a touch of contempt into his benign smile. He was a florid man with painted toes and he smoked a hashish stick in a manner at once debonair and disarming. "Are you sure?"

"Quite sure." The little man was respectfully firm.

Behind his desk, in his huge wicker chair, the psychiatrist seemed lost in thought. He gently stroked a large phallic symbol with his thumb.

"Why are you sure?" he asked at last. "How do you know that your belief in God is not the result of childhood indoctrination, or perhaps a masochistic frustration symbol, or even an expression of every man's hopeless yearning for happiness?" He was confident, brimming over with bonhomie, and the hook was twice as alluring in its naked openness. The little man was not deceived.

"I have lived long enough to know there is a God. He stops me from doing things I want to do. He lets me do things I don't want to do—and His permission amounts to an order. Oh, I know He's there all right and He has forbidden fornication."

The florid man had seized the cogent point, and clung to it.

"Then you still insist that you arc thousands of years old. Surely this seems odd to you. Other people never live much beyond a hundred. How many thousand years did you say you've been alive?"

The little man lost his composure, He was a neat little man, and did not look to be thousands of years old.

"This is the problem, of course. I can't remember. I only recall flashes, not only déjà vu but genuine memories. When I check old records, I invariably prove correct. Sometimes more correct, as investigation has shown in a couple of cases. But I keep forgetting things. In a fortnight's time I probably won't remember coming to you but if I see another psychiatrist I'll have an uneasy feeling I've done it before. To tell the truth, I have that uneasy feeling now."

He shifted in the air cushions of the couch, and snapped his mouth shut..

The florid man sucked smoke out of the stick, dribbled it into the air, and ogled the Rabelaisian painting on the far wall.

"Your problem," he said, quietly, sanely, the wild good humor of a perfectly balanced individual skimming just beneath the surface of his words, "is sexual. Which is why I suggested a sexual remedy. You quite obviously hated your parents. This is nothing to be ashamed of. It's part of the evolutionary progress. Indeed I believe your St. Paul advises quite strongly to cast off the old man. In your case you have taken a path of least resistance and forgotten your parents, at the same time placing yourself in loco parentis by devising snatches of imaginary memories which would make you older than your parents."

A lesser man would have sat back with a beam of self-congratulation, but the psychiatrist merely shifted his gaze to a voluptuously painted breast and chewed on his hashish slick.

The little man sighed sadly, and strangely enough the sigh

did sound like the gusting of an ancient wind, dry and stale and sad across a couple of thousand years. He pulled himself to a sitting position, considerably buffeted in the process by the pneumatic couch as its internal stresses rippled the couch in an exhibition of dynamic forces. Heavier men had been ruffled in the past by the behavior of the couch, and the little man was no exception. Flustered, he jumped to his feet and waved his check book helplessly. The psychiatrist's look was calculating, and a trifle tired, and he made no attempt to take advantage of the little man's embarrassment.

"All right, then, you're the paying customer." The hashish stick had vanished, and the florid man peered over plump joined fingers. "If you don't agree with my diagnosis, that's your privilege—and your loss. The only thing I can suggest if you really are set against fornication is a spot of fishing. It's the second-best thing for washing away those nasty pent-up prenatal emotions. The receptionist will take the check. Good afternoon and a cheery fixation."

The polished maple door was open, the psychiatrist was standing beside it, teeth bared and hand extended, and in a scuttling moment the little man was borne into the receptionist's office. Behind her desk she was wide and white-clad and motherly, and the little man almost waited to be picked up by the hind legs and smacked. His eyes closed, his throat moved convulsively, his signature formed on the blank check, and he fled.

Outside in the street the bright sunlight baffled his eyes. Incredible memories jumped in his mind, shouting a loud negative to the psychiatrist's forceful facile answers. The little man was tossed and pushed by the eddying currents of humanity about him, but he was oblivious to the smart people and their towering skyscrapers and their ephemeral worries. Visions, sounds and smells swirled in his mind as the crowd carried him to the subway. Automatically, he dropped his coin, passed through a turnstile. His feet took him to the fifty-mile-per-hour strip and he stood submerged in the mass of people about him, swarming in their multitude.

But he was no longer in the bustle of the twenty-first century. The myriad worlds of memory stood at his feet, and he trod them like a weary disillusioned god. Again, he walked along the great stone quays of Byblos, smelled the exotic odors of spices as heavy-limbed slaves unloaded them, caught his foot on a huge roughly hewn plank of cedar from Lebanon, cursed as a sweating soldier butted him with the haft of a short spear.

He gazed across the swelling storm waters of an unpredictable Mediterranean, sweltered in the flapping shade of a great white mainmast, fearful of the straining and grinding of the yard high above him.

He sat at the crude table of a monastery refectory, daintily picking at his food while the vulgar oafs around him wolfed down their meat with their hands and belched after their swill of wine.

He stood in one corner of a vast, elegant, over-decorated Victorian drawing room, listening to a dandy sweep delicate white hands over ivory keys in a startlingly poignant evocation of Chopin's Études.

The memories brought little satisfaction. In the blurred world of frustration and anguish about him on the speeding, creaking slideway, the little man gazed in unseeing misery. Ennui is a terrible disease, and the little man had been incubating it for several thousand years.

A large element of the little man's misery was his feeling of being lost at sea. All around him the short-lived scurrying humans dashed in their search for material comfort, clogging their minds and pores with activity in the endless race to submerge their souls. They knew whence they came; they knew that the dust of the earth would take back their bodies in less than a century. Their lives were neatly packeted, their three score and ten deftly notched with a program of sublimation which would carry them from first howl to last groan with the minimum of spiritual travail. But the little man's world had no such handy parameters. It was a chaos of a hundred past lives, and a farrago of a million possible futures.

Sometimes the little man thought he might be God.

Only sometimes, of course. He knew he was not God. God pushed him around. His thoughts of God were not bitter, though perhaps he had every right to be bitter about God. On the contrary, he was quite fond of Him. In the little man's colossal boredom, the only pleasure remaining was to try to sneak a swift move past God's eyes.

It hardly ever worked, though, and the little man came reluctantly up from his sea of memories to look about him for an opportunity to put one over God. A man sat a few feet from him, on the floor, lost in a celibate intellectual orgasm. Dopers were becoming more common as the mass mind endeavored to lose itself in the disguise of looking for itself. Further along the strip a tart in an orange and purple striped Bedouin nightie caught his eye. She wriggled her thin body, and when the little man nodded she sauntered up to him.

The little man derived a sad beaten masochistic pleasure in the anticipation of what would happen. God had forbidden fornication and if God was on the ball as He invariably was— there, with a frightened look, the little tart backed off suddenly and disappeared in a swirl of translucent color. Something in the little man's face, something in the world, but certainly not of it, something an earlier age might have associated with spectral fingers or floating Grails, something threw her back in terror. The little man followed her with his eyes, unhappily, and saw her break her leg as she stepped backwards on to a slow strip.

By the time the little man had left the strip and was making his way up an afternoon-lit suburban road, he had forgotten the psychiatrist and the thin tart had faded from memory. He walked up a quiet hill, a peaceful street of browned grass and old houses and ancient Scotty dogs. There were no children here to disturb the heavy meditative senile air, and the little man was grateful for that if nothing else. The great gables hung heavy, and ivy crept up the walls, clinging to life.

The little man was tired, tired to death, tired of life and the endless futile childish round of food and activity and sleep. He thought of the gilded Florentine palaces where he had slept, the nasal tones of Lorenzo de' Medici, the flickering rapier which had taken off his left ear and made him look lopsided before the ear grew back. He thought of the dust-ridden Californian ranch he had helped to build, when only a handful of white men had seen the Pacific from an American beach. He thought, and he thought, and he remembered the beer he had not been allowed to drink and the women he could not touch because they walked away afeared, and the money he could never keep enough of to be rich, and he was tired.

Finally, his feet were still, and he pushed his key into the front door lock and with a slight click the door opened. The house was musty, cool, empty and heartbreaking. The little man paused at the refrigerator for a glass of lemonade, went to the back room and brought in to the kitchen a fine hemp rope. Between his fingers it felt good, rough and strong, and an inch thick. He looped it, tied the loop carefully into a hangman's noose, and held it out proudly to survey it.

The kitchen was roofed with waxed boards, and a great cross plank stretched above the little man's head. Carefully, he moved a chair over and stood on it. The other end of the rope went over the huge beam and the little man knotted it with delicate precision. He pulled it, swung on it, and the rope calmly held. He slipped the noose over his head, arranged the knot carefully behind the base of his skull, and peered for the last time around the room. But he was tired, bored, and unless he put an end to his thousands of years of life soon, he would be too bored to do even that. With a sigh of gratitude, he kicked away the chair and the rough fibers of the rope cut shockingly into his throat as he fell.

The rope broke, of course, and Lazarus skinned his knee.

THE WOMB

Twice have I stood a beggar
Before the door of God!
Angels, twice descending,
Reimbursed my store.
Burglar, banker, father,
I am poor once more!

Emily Dickinson, 1858

i.

My father despised biographies, but even more (or so he told his followers) he detested movies and novels and invented stories of every kind. "Fiction is the gossip of those who don't get out much, Rosa," he told me once, with a smile. No doubt I was curled up with a book at the time. "Purveyed," he added, sarcastically, "by those who don't get out at all." So here I am writing a story, his story, perhaps my story as well, possibly the chronicle of us all. No doubt my father would laugh heartily at this. Will laugh. I don't know.

My father, after all, is the Rev. Daimon Keith who revealed to us, in the years prior to his second disappearance, that as a youth he had been abducted from the vicinity of a Clayton school playground by small gray aliens. Indeed, Daimon had been taken up into UFOs not just that once, in Australia, at the age of twenty, but from infancy, and over and again. No doubt it was this germinal and outlandish experience that caused him to devote his middle years to the establishment of the Church of Jesus Christ, Time Traveller (or, as the American chapters have it, "Traveler"), and later Scionetics. At last, as his madness grew deeper and more hilarious, its equivocal memory fetched him to the belief that it was his own Nazarene face which the black-eyed aliens had sculpted from a eroded mesa on the surface of Mars, memorialized so ambiguously in the famous 1976 NASA photographs and twenty-two years later so conclusively unmasked, despite his angry blustering, as my father's fame neared its zenith.

To exist in the shadow—the dark aura, perhaps—of such a father is, you might suppose, inevitably to grow up as a wretch obliged to launch the tale of her own life with details of her father's name and lunatic obsessions. Do not think to find me out so readily. My life has not been so straightforward, nor is Daimon's notoriety altogether just. I am a student of narrative, as are we all in these early days of the millennium, fully up to the mark with anxieties of influence. I have every intention of constructing and revising my father's testament, if only I can find my way to the bottom of it. For now perhaps a sketch must suffice, or a series of arbitrary laminations.

You should know at once that for a long time I understood that he tried to force my mother to have an abortion (or so I was told frequently) and, when she refused in horror, attempted to give me up for adoption three days after my birth, which he would inform his followers had occurred on July 20, 1969, a little after midday, Eastern Australian Time. This, the elderly among you might recall, was the moment Neil Armstrong set his foot upon the Moon, during the first landing by the Apollo astronauts. In fact, I was not born until the middle of 1975, and the gap serves my father's purposes admirably, for people are always taken by how young I seem. It is a subtly tacit endorsement of his esoteric teachings.

His own birthdate is hardly less notable, for Daimon entered the world—by his own account—on August 6, 1945, within hours of that other Little Boy who squalled into heat and light over Hiroshima. An untrustworthy natal date.

One last prefatory point: although his family and friends call my father "Deems," a childhood nickname, his proper given name is not pronounced "Demon," as the ignoramuses of the mass media assume, but "Die-moan," in the way of its Greek source. If that vulgar error was an occasion of chagrin for a man of the cloth, even cloth so self-elected and flamboyant as my father's, he never allowed his family to perceive it. His name had been gifted to him from his Scottish grandfather, a classicist of minor note in the Ballarat gold fields, and it means, as you may know already, a kind of indwelling spirit or force of nature. Certainly he became that for his daughter, even as Daimon became convinced that he himself was now infested by illuminations from beyond the present: from beyond the world itself.

For all that, I am not Rosa Keith but Rosa Rosch, named fore and aft by my mother Margaret, the strong-willed woman who stole me away me from his clutches when I was five years old.

ii.

Aboard the Zetan craft

In his dreaming confusion, he knew that it had started again. The musty stench reminded him of mice, the piles and heaps of mouse droppings they'd found in his uncle's empty weekender when they'd gone to Queenscliff for a cheap winter holiday. The bench he lay on was not quite hard, and the long, lighted oblong above his head burned like a pink musk-stick sucked to a piercing sweetness in the vacant eternities of geometry and geography classes. His dry tongue searched his mouth for the absent taste. The brothers would snatch the candy from his mouth if they found him enjoying it during a lesson. Once, Brother Ronald had literally seized his jaw in one handball-roughened fist and pinched the nerves, forcing the nub of musk-stick out from between his teeth, made him spit it on to the scratched school desk. In the pink darkness, as his heart accelerated with the fright of being here once again, he felt a quirky grin move his lips, at that memory within a dream, because at least Brother Ronald isn't around to torment him.

Something was standing at his side. Something like a doll formed hastily from putty and not left long enough in the sun, moist and pliant, curvy and dirty white. He could not bring himself to turn and look at it. Yet the disgust he felt seemed, somehow, to come from the creature itself. There was another of them at the foot of the slab, with its blobby head and wrap-around eyes, doing something to his left foot. That was hard to understand, because normally he was very ticklish. If one of the guys grabbed his bare foot, he'd go into a girlish paroxysm of giggles and flailing around. The thing down there was fooling with his foot, and it wasn't making him giggle one little bit. Quite the contrary. He felt sick with anxiety, and numb, and heavy in the limbs.

He screamed, then, a hard sharp yelp, as a needle went into the flesh between his big toe and the next toe along.

"Hey! Cut it out!"

In the funny atmosphere, his words hung in his ears like underwater echoes. Had he even spoken?

"Fuck!" The bastard was shoving the fucking needle deeper into his god-damned foot! "Jesus!"

This was unbelievable. Every time he came here they did something like this. And every time he told them how much it hurt, how vehemently he detested their invasion of his private places, but it never made the slightest bit of difference. Never did the faintest bit of good. But they were not cruel, he knew that. The one at his side touched his forehead with a cool tube, it felt like, something glimmery and pale, not metal and not plastic, and it soothed him at once. It took away the pain. No, the pain was still there, but it didn't hurt any more. Did that make any sense? It was like shoving with your tongue at a dead tooth. That baby tooth he'd pried at with his fingers and his tongue for a week and half, deciduous tooth they call it, when he was seven years old. He'd even tried that old trick they tell you about, loads of laughs, cheaper than a visit to the dentist, and you got your lucrative visit from the tooth fairy that much sooner. You tied a piece of string around the loose tooth and attached the end to a door knob, and another kid jerked the door open and out popped your floppy baby tooth. It hadn't worked. It had hurt like blazes, and the string tightened and cut into his gum, and he got his backside tanned when Mum came in from the back yard, drawn by his yelping and howling, and found him with this bloody string hanging out of his god-damned bleeding gum like he'd been gargling with a tampon or something.

Deliberately, he turned his head and stared at the putty-gray creature at his side.

Look away! the gray thing told him in his mind. Stop staring at me! You know we don't like you looking at us!

He averted his gaze, feeling horribly guilty, as if he'd been caught staring through a crack in the wall into some girl's bathroom while she was taking a pee or something. Which he had done, now that he thought about it, back in that old dairy they'd had in Olive Street, Jesus, how incredible, he'd been 11 or 12 and they still ladled out fresh creamy milk into washed bottles you brought from home there to the dairy, right in the middle of the suburbs, well, okay, out on the edge of the metropolitan area, but still. And there were milkman's delivery horses, was that right? Hairy hoofed big bastards, sweet natured and much given to shitting placidly and copiously right there in the street. His father made him rush out after they'd been past, carrying a flat-bladed spade and a hessian sack, to scoop up the steaming, heavy-smelling horse crap and bag it for the garden, God, he'd been so embarrassed, none of the neighbors did that, they probably thought his father was a perv of some kind, a manure fancier, maybe they thought we ate it with our milk and white sugar and Weeties.

Get up, the alien told him. We have to go now.

He seemed to float in an amazingly heavy way. They went

across the curved brushed-aluminum floor toward the huge curving windows full of stars, and there was a door in the wall but it wasn't actually a door, it wasn't even marked as a door, they went through it without its opening, holy shit! He had just passed through the fucking wall like smoke. No, as if the wall was smoke. Curdled for a moment. Floating. There was that strange stink again. What do these guys eat? With mouths like that, how could they eat anything? Maybe they sucked blood through a straw. And here was that room again, that hallway, full of green-gold tubes in serried ranks. Each was twice the height of a tall man, and inside each there hung a human body, male and female alike, naked, long-haired. Their eyes were closed as if they slept, or were dead. In the green medium they floated, as he floated down the corridor in their midst, and their long hair streamed out from their scalps.

It was too awful to be borne. He squeezed his eyes shut tightly, and looked away.

Good boy, he thought he heard. Do not look. They are just dolls. But he secretly turned his head again and squinted at the ranks of drowned people and his heart squeezed hard and bumped. The tubes were not as large as he'd supposed, not by a long chalk. They were much closer than he had imagined, and they were smaller than the gray dwarfs leading him in their midst. They were hardly larger than test tubes, if the truth be known, and the creatures floating in them—pale, stringy haired, barely sexed—were like fetuses, limbs slightly curved, bobbing in the liquid that preserved them. The horrid little things were less alien than the gray bastards, but certainly less human than anyone he'd ever seen. In fact they looked like some kind of unholy hybrid, some vile intermixing of the two species. He wanted to scream or vomit or reach out and tear things apart in his rage, but he could not move, and the wall parted without opening and he was in his bed again.

He lay staring at the familiar ceiling for a moment, while the pounding of his heart subsided, and waited for sound to resume. A car went by in the street, throwing the edges of its headlights through the closed louvers, and he looked fearfully around the room through slitted eyes without opening them properly. The putty-gray creature stood there still, on the other side of the bed.

As always, something prevented him from screaming blue murder and waking his parents. Anyway, they had to know about this. Jesus, it had been going on as long as he could remember. Two years old, three? Up in the sky, in the blue gushing light beam, drawn toward the clouds and the shining disk, and his parents sitting frozen on the grass in the back yard, beer glasses in their hands, smiling at each other. They hadn't helped. Or was that when he was six, just back from the hospital after getting his tonsils out? There'd been a polio scare that year, and they'd kept him in the private hospital to see he was okay, and during the night the gray Harvesters had come and lifted him and three of the other kids out of the ward. Nobody ever did anything to stop them, not your parents and not your teachers, nor even the brisk nurses or the doctors, the human doctors, that is. Adults were useless, really. They'd let you get fucked up the arse in front of their very eyes and they wouldn't lift a finger to help.

iii.

20 July 1999, San Diego

My father, Commodore the Reverend Daimon Keith of the spacetime cruiser *Zygote*, sits at ease behind a desk of audio-visual controls. Scionetics devotees face him, cross-legged on cushions. A Saint-Saëns symphony, rendered soft and luminous for New Age sensibilities, fills the room's acoustic background like an odor of cinnamon. At the back of my balding, silver-haired father, on a huge bank of high definition TV screens, a ceaseless montage lifts the hearts of his followers, placing Deems in his proper context: sweet pale Australian sky with little white merino sheep clouds, rust-red outback dunes, the soaring, ancient curve of Uluru like a stone fallen from heaven, the Moon's cratered surface seen from the window of Armstrong's plummeting Lunar Excursion Module thirty years ago to the day, deep heaven itself captured by the Hubble telescope, black as eternity, roaring with a violence of stars and quasar plumes a hundred or a thousand light years in extent. Deems is clad appropriately in his commodore's uniform, silver jump suit cinched at the waist, emblazoned on shoulder and breast with the curiously aching symbols he and his fellow abductees have seen etched into the curved walls of UFO operating theatres. When he speaks to his followers, though, there is no hint of grandiosity or vainglory. This is a man among men and women, a seeker after truth, a witness to the incredible among us.

"Friends," he says quietly, and his relaxed words are captured and borne lightly by hidden speakers to every ear, "let's talk today about one of the oldest questions of philosophy: the meaning of life. You'll be relieved to learn that I have an answer to this question," he says with a smile, to a ripple of quiet amusement, "although it would not please the philosophers who first sought its resolution, nor the dreary men and women of today's academies who lack the wisdom or even the curiosity to ask it. I can give you a complete and provable four-word answer to that question, What is the meaning of human life? But my concise reply might merely shock and disturb you, friends, unless we first go carefully through the reasoning that leads us to this revelation—the revelation of the gray harvesters who brought me to its understanding."

"Tell us anyway," cries a fervent voice.

"We're up for it, man," cries another.

Deems gazes at them sardonically. "Really? You actually think you can handle this revelation?"

"Sure."

A little voice pipes, "You'll help us understand it," and everyone laughs, friendly and enthusiastic.

"I will indeed, Sandra," Daimon says with a smile. He leans forward, putting his silver elbows on the desk. "Very well, let's take a chance here. What is the meaning of life? The philosophers and theologians and shamans and public relations flacks struggled with this one for thousands of years. I'm here to tell you, friends, that their answers aren't worth a pinch of shit. We can forget them. The speculations of Plato and Aquinas and Kant about the meaning of human life were exactly as informed and interesting as their speculations about nuclear physics. It's not just that they were wrong about everything that science has since revealed to us. It's not just that their guesses were childishly primitive. No, friends, they weren't even asking the right questions. Which is why the answer to that big question, that ultimate question, seems so hard for us to accept. Until we see through it, and through the question. Here's the answer, friends."

He pauses. They crane forward. Surely they have heard this before, know it as their catechism, but the thrill never leaves them, the burst of creepy shock, that exultant shock of freedom and transgression and sheer good humor in Daimon's UFO revelation.

"What is the meaning of human life? It is the same answer the wise scientist gives if asked, What is the meaning of the sun? What is the meaning of a tidal wave that smashes a hundred thousand suffering people caught in its path? What is the meaning of the sky's darkness at night? What is the meaning of a joyful orgasm that begins a new life?"

He stands up abruptly, and the great screen at his back goes scarlet, a shocking explosion of blood or sunset, and then to utter black. In the center of the void, a tiny flower of piercing light opens. Its petals unfold. It is the universe in the first moments of creation, the Big Bang itself, the universe uttered into existence. Organ chords carry the numinous message. Daimon stands before them, his silvery suit catching light from the screen. He is exultant, and he stares at them with absolute conviction.

"What is the meaning of human life?

"There is no meaning."

July, 2005, Los Angeles

After my mother was slaughtered, butchered and eaten by Valentine the guru and his followers, I spent the next ten years submitting at night to physical and sexual abuse by members of Harmonic Resonance and studying tensely at a cult school during the day. This is hardly the place to dilate upon that atrocious decade, which I blocked from conscious memory until my chance encounter with Benjamin Thompson, Daimon's adopted son.

By 2003, my step-brother was an established therapist in the USA specializing in deep recovery techniques, having broken some years earlier with the Church of Jesus Christ, Time Traveler (as it was known on the West Coast) after my father denounced his earlier claims and slid the movement's substantial holdings into a Malaysian account for the newly announced Scionetics organization.

My own powers of recall were in terrible shape, of course, for I had developed a barrage of dissociative personality disorders to permit me to cope, however inadequately, with my rough handling by the Harmonic Resonance cultists. It was my belief, until Ben opened up the hideous can of worms under my skull, that Margaret Rosch had died in an automobile accident six months after our arrival in the United States, and that I had been adopted by her ditzy friend Katie, whom I called "Mom" from that day hence.

The most curious aspect of this hidden life is that Benjamin had no slightest inkling of our familial relationship when the hypnotic probing began in his comfortable Los Angeles office, or of the type of banal horror he would unmask. From all the indicator instruments I filled out tediously, a barrage of Minnesota Multiphasic Personality Inventories, Hopkins Image Recognition Test cards, Barber Suggestibility Indices and so on, he had expected that I was a prime candidate for alien abductee of the year.

It was not true; to the best of my knowledge I have never been visited by the gray gynecologists, never gone into their high laboratories for probing and ovary pillage. I'm sure that's true. When I came out of trance, Benjamin sat looking at me with a very pale and bemused expression. His obese black nurse busied herself with the Mac voice-activated transcriber, a machine prone to lexical ambiguity unless watched closely, and her matronly presence protected both of us from any possible subsequent forensic disputes.

I could remember little of my hypnotic testimony. "Was I abducted by a UFO?" I asked my new therapist hopefully. Anything was better than this awful *not knowing*.

He coughed, and coughed again. Something seemed to be stuck in his throat, and I doubt that it was an alien implant.

"Your name is not Angel," he told me, evading my question, "it's Rosa. Rosa Rosch."

No, my lost life did not instantly flood back into my conscious awareness like a dam bursting. I looked at him as if he were the one with the mental problem.

"What?"

Benjamin sat where he was and extended his beautiful hand to within 20 centimeters of my own. "May I hold your hand?"

I gave my permission. His grip was warm and firm, if, I thought, a trifle damp. He was anxious. His eyes darted about my face.

"Rosa, you are my step-sister."

I withdrew my hand and got smartly off the couch. "Send me your bill," I said coldly, making for the door. The nurse somehow got in my way, and Benjamin reached past her and took my hand again, increasing his grip.

"They did terrible things to you, Angel," he said. "They took away your mother, and your name, and your history, and your peace of mind. But at least they were not able to harm the rest of your family. We thought you were gone for good, Rosa." There were genuine tears in his eyes. "If you wish to see your father, I can arrange a meeting."

I was thunderstruck.

"My father? Don't be silly, Dr. Thompson, my father died many years ago."

"No," Benjamin told me, with a smile, "your father is alive and kicking."

"Who is he?" I forced myself to ask, through lips anaesthetized with fear and hope. This man was clearly out of his tree. Dr. Ben placed credence, after all, in the routine abduction and pillage of a tenth of the population of these United States, so he was patently unhinged. But then I was slowly remembering, through a numb, shaking haze, the details of the regression: that my mother had been hacked up and stir-fried by sweet-natured people, my own extended mystical family, who claimed to be vegetarians.

"Your father is quite a famous fellow," Benjamin told me, with a certain ambiguous satisfaction. It is hard to dislike Deems, after all. "The Reverend Daimon Keith, founder of Scionetics."

We had not been permitted to read the *National Enquirer* at Harmony, nor indeed watch vulgar television programs, and after my escape I had never gotten into the habit. I didn't have a clue what he was talking about.

v.

August 1970, inside the UFO

He opened his eyes, and it was happening again. Were they under the bed, hiding beneath the fall of the blankets? Were they peeking at him from the crack of the closet's open door? Were they lurking behind the door? No. The door was closed, it was deep in the middle of the night. Everyone else in the house was asleep. He wanted to huddle into the comforting warmth of body-heated sheets and covers, but somehow they had been pulled away. It was cold. He felt so cold that he was sure he must be shivering, but his legs and arms were so heavy that he could not even shiver. They were standing there next to his bed, looking at him with their huge dark eyes.

"Go away," he said, wanting to scream.

They were just out of view, at the edges of his vision. Were there four of them, or five? The gray doctor was one of them, he could tell that much. They would do things to him again. Within his chilled, heavy flesh, his heart thudded. One thin hand came up over the edge of the bed and touched his own bare hand with a metal rod. He yelped, once, and then his heart slowed, calmed.

"What?" he asked sluggishly. "What?"

He was to go with them once more. They meant to put him on their ship and invade his body again. Despite the effects of the rod, his blood seemed to cool even further. His stomach contracted in fear. Light poured suddenly from the wall between his bedroom and the backyard. The small gray people, dirty-white people, big-eyed bugs without mouths or noses passed into the light with jerky, spasmodic steps. Like frames of a badly-edited old film. Jump cuts. Merging into each other like some sort of overlap. He was in the air and moving into the blue light.

It was so cold. The light was gone. He lay tilted on his side somehow, the blood draining into the left side of his face and body. The slab was hard, unyielding. Yes, they had brought him into the round room again. He recognized the heavy stink of the place. What do they eat? he thought blurrily. What kind of awful crap do they suck up through those lipless little mouths? The gray doctor touched his forehead with a needle. It was sharp, long, glinting in the dimness. The doctor pushed it hard into his skull, like a drill, and it hurt. It was agonizing! He could not believe that they were doing this to him again. The sadistic bastards. Don't they know anything about pain? He told himself that he would teach them about pain if they let him loose, if they withdrew this sickening heaviness from his arms and legs. Tears flooded his closed eyes.

"Why are you resisting?" asked the one he called Klar-2.

"It hurts so much," he whimpered. The needle came out of his cranium now and, without cleaning it, the gray doctor put it up into his left nostril. A blob of blood and gray goo clung to the needle as it went deep into his nose. He wished he could faint, or just die. The pain was excruciating, and they would not let him scream or turn away. The needle drilled and drilled, and a stench of burning entered the whole of his head like a ponderous cloud. Out came the needle, the drill, and one of the others handed Klar-2 a long flexible tube with a three-clawed grip at its snout. The gray doctor pushed the new thing up into his nostril. Light burst through his head, and for a moment he did lose consciousness. Despite the torpor they had induced in him, he convulsed in agony as the device came out of his nose. Blearily, he saw that its tiny claw now held a small burred sphere. Klar-2 held it up for general inspection. A drop of blood fell from the device. The gray doctor's eyes were huge and dark, a brown almost black. Throbbing, burning pain hung in his head.

Two of the small aliens took him by the hand, one on each side. The slab rotated until it stood vertical, and then, to his horror and disbelief, it swiveled forward another thirty or forty degrees. He dangled above them, unsupported. This was not free-fall, not a region of the ship without gravity. From time-lapsed moment to moment he felt dizzily that he might fall and smash his nose—his tender, brutalized nose!—on the segmented metal deck. Instead he somehow remained stuck to the hard surface while they inspected him with their gadgets, their stupid toys. He realized suddenly that he was so cold because they had stripped him naked. At the same moment, one of them touched his penis with its machine. To his horror, he instantly got an erection. His rage increased.

"You bastards! Leave me alone, you shits."

They stepped aside into shadows, and the slab whirled back to the horizontal. He lay, heavy, immobile, with his ridiculous hard-on sticking straight up at the lens or light or whatever it was on the ceiling. Out of the corner of his eye he saw a seamless doorway open in the wall to his left, close again. A woman in a silvery cloak and long stringy pale hair came into the chamber, and the aliens did their jump-cut retreat as she approached the slab.

His humiliation was complete. The woman was not quite human, but there was no telling his fucking mindless dick that. It quivered, a randy jolt that was not quite an ejaculation. He remembered that they had done this before. They had brought some kind of tube over and connected it to his penis as if he were a prize bull, and he'd spurted his jism into it even as he had roared his furious rejection of them. Everything blurred. Cliché or not, this had to be a nightmare, a dream, the sort of fantasy you get when you've gone over the edge, cracked up; a stupid, unbelievable image dredged from horror movies.

Something light and cool touched his right eyelid, and he realized that he had been lying hunched with his eyes tightly clamped shut. The pale-haired woman regarded him without expression. She touched her own garment twice, at throat and groin, and it fell from her. Somehow, crumpled, it flew across the room and stuck to the side of the chamber.

She pushed him off the slab.

The metal floor struck his shoulder, and his left ankle clipped the hard edge of the slab as he fell. Emotions collided inside him: outrage and hilarity. He lay on the slick floor, rubbing his ankle, and started to laugh. He pushed himself to a standing position, conscious of his absurd hard-on, and looked over his stinging shoulder at the woman.

She had got herself on to the slab and lay there looking expressionlessly at the ceiling lens. Naked and unpleasant as a fish, she was stretched out like someone expecting a disagreeable medical examination. The gray doctor touched his arm, and he jumped. Where had that bastard come from?

You will give her a baby, Klar-2 instructed him in the weird way they had, without opening his slitty mouth.

"Fuck you!"

There was perhaps the faintest tinge of ironic amusement in

the alien's gaze. Impossible. It was *alien*!

He looked back at the woman. At least she was human. Sort of. Her hair was long and unappealing, Alice in Wonderland grown up a bit. On the face of it she should have been attractive, but something about her rigid presence repelled him. Her breasts were small, but sagged a little. Her public hair was thick, untrimmed. She saw him looking at her and opened her legs, lifting her knees. The gray doctor gave him a push in the back.

"Forget it!"

But a kind of sexual pulse passed through him, a perverse pleasure at this insanely obscene spectacle. What, they abduct you into a fucking flying saucer and stick needles up your nose and drill your brain, and then they expect you to bang some hybrid alien? Jesus! His erection could not make up its mind. Klar-2 struck him more firmly in the small of his back, and the lights on the control patches around the walls began to fizz and flicker. He had not noticed any lights earlier, or any control surfaces.

The slab was now twice its previous width, a narrow double bed for a celestial wedding. Christ! He approached the woman hesitantly, and let his hand fall on her ribcage. His erection was sagging. Her flesh had never seen sunlight and seemed slightly moist. With a sigh, he clambered on to the slab and lay next to her. There was no response. He played for a moment with her stringy hair, touched one small nipple briefly, sent his fingers down between her legs. She failed to react to his caresses. He licked his fingers and tried again. A sour, faintly rank odor rose from her body as her cunt moistened. He hoisted himself dutifully over her supine body and tried to enter her, but his erection had subsided.

To his amazement, he found himself muttering, "I'm sorry."

The woman looked at him, looked away.

"Just a moment."

He tried to kiss her, and her mouth remained closed and unresponsive. Humiliated, he lay like a log on her.

"It might help if I knew your name," he said.

Cinder, she told him. Had he heard her correctly? A cold demon from hell? The Cinderella of the flying saucers? Was he the prince, then, trying to fit his foot into her glass slipper? Foot: ha! Inch was more like it. But her name fired something in him. His hard-on half returned. He touched her, touched himself, forced himself somehow into her. The gray doctor was watching them with his awful black owl's eyes, and nudged him at the base of the spine with a device. Whimpering, he came in a thin trickle.

He lay exhausted and sick at heart on the slab as she got carefully to her feet and dressed again in the silver garment. "Why won't you tell me anything about yourselves?" he asked bitterly. "Who the hell are you people? How dare you use us like this?"

We have transferred our souls, bodies and minds into computer implementation and moved millions of light-years back into your time dimension, the Cinder creature told him coldly. Our command center is in another dimension beyond the supposed god you call the sun. We are millions of light-years backwards. The voice you are hearing has been sent billions of light-years ahead.

"I don't understand," he said, sitting up and hugging himself. He felt sticky and abused. "What is this bullshit? "Light-years" isn't time, it's a distance. A schoolchild could tell you that."

In the singularity metric, the gray doctor informed him, time and space are unitary.

"You mean a black hole?"

One little point collapses all dimensions, the woman told him. Powers gather through that point. It is the main channel for tuning into worlds with greater probability.

"Dimensions? Like, time and space? You mean time and space vanish when you go through a black hole? Is that how you get here?"

The accumulation of time does not vanish. You must understand that space with an infinite rotational energy tensor excludes time. We gather it in and put it to work. Our devices are using up time.

He did not understand. He sat there on the slab, downcast and tired and sad, and waited for them to send him back in their beams of light.

vi.

FILM MAKER SNATCHED BY LITTLE GRAY MEN
BY JUDITH FRIPP (Melbourne, Tuesday)

In 1952, Californian guru and café handy man George Adamski snapped a flying saucer and met the ski instructor from Venus who drove it. In 1975, timber worker Travis Walton was "abducted" by aliens for five days. Two years ago, Australian pilot Frederick Valentich vanished at sea after his plane was buzzed by a UFO, and hasn't been seen since. Now it's the turn of slick ad man and director Damon Keith, 35 (photo at right), to vacation on Venus.

Anyway, that's the explanation from his step-son, Ben Thompson, who watched them take Damon in a blue beam of light. Ben's real father is the famous cinematographer Vic Thompson, now working in Europe and the US with Peter Weir and Fred Schepisi among other ex-pat luminaries of local cinema. His worried mother Zelda, the former Mrs. Thompson, is now married to Damon. Confused?

The vanished Mr. Keith is known in Melbourne's bohemian arts circles for some entertaining pranks played when he was a comic turn and anti-Vietnam activist at Carlton's La Mama and Pram Factory theatres.

St. Kilda police were not commenting on the bizarre abduction claim, although they stated that Mr. Keith had been listed routinely as a missing person. By a strange coincidence, Mr. Keith recently returned from California, after an unsuccessful search for his daughter. Five-year-old Rosa was allegedly taken to the USA without his permission by her unmarried mother, Ramona M. Roach.

An officer warned that anybody making a false statement to police could be charged and prosecuted. No UFOs were booked in the bayside suburb for exceeding the speed of light on the rainy Saturday night.

Some late night disco revelers made independent reports of a "bright disc" hovering below the clouds near Luna Park. A local astronomer said this was "almost certainly" a shooting star, or meteor.

Ben Thompson, 18, admits he has been a "flying saucer nut" since childhood, when he believes he himself was contacted by creatures from outer space. He can even tell you where they come from—a planet called Zeeta Reticule!

Asked when he expects his step-father to return from his Spielberg adventure (remember *Close Encounters of the Third Kind*?), the second-year psychology student said he feared for Mr. Keith's life. "They killed Captain Mandell," he said, referring to a famous jet pilot who crashed while chasing what US authorities say was a weather balloon.

And who are these little gray men? Aren't they meant to be green? A common error, says Ben. The UFO guys (and sexy gals!) come in plenty of shapes and colors, but strangely enough hardly any of them are green.

Anyone sighting Mr. Keith on the ground is asked to contact St Kilda police, who will notify his concerned family.

vii.

4 January 2000, Langley interrogation unit 8

Despite the clamor and frenzy caused by my father's second disappearance, he had not been abducted yet again by the Zetans. On the contrary, he seethed in a massively secure apartment (call it a cell and you would not be far wrong) in Maryland, USA. Every night he was fed well, given access to a superior choice of cable first release movies, permitted to swim or exercise in a compact but comprehensive gymnasium, all in the company of one pert young woman or another, each of whom made it clear that as part of her duties she was happy to stay the night in his king-size bed. Every morning he was fed an ample breakfast and then taken to a stark white room and attached to myographs and other stress-indicator devices, and asked by a fresh team his opinions about UFOs, world politics, and the meaning of life.

"I'm writing a new book," he told his fourth pair of inter-rogators peevishly. "Look in my notebook, there's a directory called *The Zygote Paradigm*."

A red-headed CIA scientist with a kindly expression flicked through his notebook menu and accessed a file. "I have it here, Mr. Keith. Do you actually expect us to believe this?"

"I couldn't give a flying fuck. Believe what you like."

Nobody slapped him heavily about the chops. The moni-toring equipment did not fry his nerves with an overdose of amps. Spiegle, a fat psychiatrist who hardly spoke during the first couple of hours of their interview, sat back in his easy chair, scratched his well-tailored belly, sighed. Tanner, the red-haired man, said, "Mr. Keith, if what you claim is true, this is the most momentous news since the discovery of the wheel."

My father stared at him, and then away, drolly, to an imagi-nary or perhaps a hidden camera. He knew that much already.

"Tell us about their propulsion system."

"Do you know how a bicycle derailleur gear system works?"

"What?"

"Have you ever ridden a bike?"

"Is this one of your cracker-barrel parables, Mr. Keith?"

"I'm an Australian, Dr. Tanner," my father told him. "If you're going to insult me, you might at least use an Australian epithet. Ask me if I'm pissing in your pocket, for example. Ask me if I'm bullshitting you. Don't bother, I'm not. It's true, every word, and if you don't believe me you can check with Sir Lindsay Taggard."

Incredibly, they had it on file. "The public servant you hoaxed back in April, 1972? I don't think he'd give you a sterling reference, Mr. Keith."

"Call me Daimon, for Christ's sake. Call me Deems. We're old pals by now, aren't we?" He had never seen them before this morning, nor had the previous pairs of interrogators shown their faces once they'd left the room.

"What *about* bike gears?"

"Have you ridden one lately? A trail bike, say, with a lovely little set of ten or twelve gears to get you up the side of the mountain."

"Not lately, but yes. So?"

"How do the derailleurs work?"

"Why, they— There's a sprocket, and the chain— I don't know. Is that what you're saying? That we leave that kind of detail to the mechanic in the store?"

"That's what I'm saying. It's metric defects, and beyond that they send it back under warranty."

The psychiatrist eased forward, lit a cigarette, blew its smoke carefully away from Daimon. "Sorry, I know you hate this, but I get stressed, okay? And we're paying for this place, Daimon. Why do you called them 'Zetans' when you know they couldn't possibly be from Zeta Reticuli?"

Deems smiled at him with admiration. "I thought you were the strong silent type. Are you telling me that Betty Hill invented her star map?"

This was an old, old story in UFO lore. When Barney Hill and his wife were kidnapped by the gray gynecologists, Betty was shown a holographic map of linked stars. Several years later a school teacher named Marjory Fish painstakingly built a scale model of the sun-like stars within 65 light years of Earth, and peered at it until she found a configuration closely matching Betty's hypnotic reproduction of the alien map.

The red-haired physicist snapped down the screen of his notebook. "You dealt with this Zeta crap yourself in that dumb Jesus book of yours, Deems. Fish would have done just as well if she'd turned Hill's dots upside down and hooked the lines together that way. Besides, the Zeta Reticuli binaries are too young and gravitationally destabilizing to have habitable planets."

My father said happily, "I love it when I see you buggers bite. 'Zetan' is a coinage of my own. It has nothing to do with the Fish map. See, the stuff the UFO aliens are built out of is cosmological dark matter, 'Zed-nought' weakly interacting particles. I suppose you illiterate Americans would say 'Zee-zero.' That's why they live near the core of the Earth where the gravity is nice and cozy. So they're Zed-Terrans—Zetans, okay?"

While the physicist had no ready reply to this, the psychiatrist was clearly disappointed; he had expected better of a man of my father's evident intelligence. "I *see*. So you subscribe to the Hollow Earth theory?"

Daimon was disappointed in return.

"Jesus, Spiegle, use your fucking ears. If the Earth was hollow, why would gravity-eaters choose to live there?"

The physicist winked at his colleague. "He's right, Leo. If his aliens are made of WIMPs or even WILPs, they'd sink straight down to the middle of the earth. Or the sun, for that matter. Do they live on the sun, Daimon?"

"*In* the sun, Tanner. Why else do you think every culture in history has worshipped the sun and the stars?"

"Well, light and warmth might have something to do with it, don't you think?"

"Uh huh, sure." My father got up and went to the nice little kitchen, where an espresso machine burbled quietly. He pulled the handle and steamy coffee spurted. "Anyone else while I'm up?"

Tanner raised his arm. "And some cookies."

"What are WILPs?" murmured the psychiatrist.

"WIMPS are weakly interacting massive particles," the physicist muttered back, "and WILPs are weakly interacting light particles. Not to be confused with photons, which are just light particles." He smirked, obscurely pleased with himself.

"The Zetans are the closest thing we can conceive to spirits," Deems told them, carrying his coffee back into the bleak room, a tall pile of biscuits balanced precariously. "So you see, Heaven turns out to be there in both directions—down below, where the priests told us Hell was, and up above, in the stars."

"You think these aliens are sort of like ghosts?" Spiegle asked grudgingly, "discarnate human souls?"

Daimon laughed out loud, a trifle hysterically.

"No, you don't have a soul, Spiegle," he said, sputtering his coffee. "Neither do you, Tanner. Sorry."

"Oh, I see, only you gifted UFO abductees have souls, right?"

"No, you fuck-wit. Did they lock your brains up when they gave you this damned jailers' job? Of course I don't have a soul, I'm an adult. Do I look like a first trimester fetus to you?"

The psychiatrist seemed taken aback. He opened his mouth, thought better of it, mused in silence. My father ate his chocolate cookie. Spiegle said slowly, "And that's why the occupants look like pre-term humans? They're neotenized, is that it? They remain somehow in the human fetal stage, but develop into a different kind of adulthood. Maybe sexless, even."

"Exactly. They are our children. Without us, there wouldn't be any of them."

"Our children grow up and become us," the physicist pointed out uneasily.

"Not all of them," Deems said. "Not those that miscarry in the womb. Not the abortions. Not the ones the Zetans engender and pilfer from the uterus of an abducted woman. And there's a lot of it going around, trust me. Put your wife under hypnosis and ask her. Or your daughters."

Both interrogators looked back at him without noticeable emotion, although there was the faintest tinge of abhorrence in the physicist's voice. "So. UFO aliens are the souls of the aborted."

"To be precise, they're the WILP complexity-correlates of the human fetal central nervous system," Daimon told them, as he had told the others like them during the past week. Nobody listened. Nothing he said seemed to get cross-indexed from one interrogation team to the next. Someone further up the chain of command was insulating this knowledge. And who could wonder at it? This was appalling news, after all. This was diabolical news. This, clearly, was why the truth about UFOs had never been made public, and never would be, not by the political and spiritual princes of the world. The Zetans, in one grotesque and illuminating revelation, had snatched away the foundations of human self-esteem, aspiration, had snatched away meaning itself.

"This is insane," the physicist said angrily. "You're telling us that another kind of evolution is going on, parallel to the universe of quarks and leptons and photons and gravitons. And you want us to accept that the sorry accidents of reproduction, the genetic waste, the biological excess, the mutations, the discards—that these are the heirs of the Kingdom of God?"

"That's what your favorite scriptures tell you," Deems said flatly. He really did not care any longer if they believed him, if they listened, if they paid attention. The gray proctologists would find him, even here under fifteen floors of subterranean steel and concrete, and lift him away to their gassy white operation rooms. The little shits were probably here right now, he thought, sitting in the middle of their air which was the heavy crust of the visible earth, listening in their puzzled way to this dreary exchange between three animals without souls.

"How could an ecology like that evolve before humans invented abortion?" Tanner said, still angry, getting angrier. "Is spiritual progress so swift that they developed their nifty starships in the ten thousand years since the invention of the...what, Leo? What did the Paleolithic sluts use to scrape themselves out? Gnawed twigs?"

Unexpectedly, the psychiatrist spoke to him sharply. "Control yourself, Professor Tanner." Spiegle met Daimon's gaze steadily. "They taught us in medical school that spontaneous human abortions account for up to eighty percent of all conceptions. I've always wondered why a replicating system shaped by evolutionary pressures would be so wasteful of metabolic energy and ecological resources."

"Well." Deems shrugged. "The *real* question is, why do so many of us go to term and live our pointless lives? But remnant life does have its useful side, you see. We're their parents, and they have to keep us on our toes. Darwin was right in his limited way. The cockroaches haven't beaten us yet in the Red Queen's Race. Or the retroviruses. All those other creepy little fuckers at the top of the food chain."

"What Red Queen?"

"He means the evolutionary arms race. One species gets smarter or quicker or more wired, and then all the others have to hustle to keep up in the same spot. My God. Abortions. Negative reincarnation. This is, this is...." The government's man looked at him with detestation. "This is techno-gnosticism."

Deems gave a yell of laughter. "I like that! Techno-gnosticism! I'll use it in my next book." Suddenly he hurled his empty coffee cup violently across the room, where it smashed on a white wall. The fragments lay curled on the tan carpet like thin ceramic fingers. "If you sons of bitches ever let me out of here."

viii.

From Rev. Daimon Keith, *The Scionetic Paradigm*, Chapter 13, "The Meaning of Life," Los Angeles: Jerome Tarcher, 2002.

Perhaps by this point some of you will have a few doubts about the truth of what I have written, or even about my sanity! Despite widespread reports of UFO abductions, despite the eerily common elements recorded in hundreds of cases worldwide, many people continue to attribute this testimony to fraud, hysteria, substance abuse or mental breakdown. Some psychiatric specialists believe the experience is caused by a brain disorder known as "transient temporal lobe dysfunction."

I have no argument with these skeptics, for I spent several years examining such explanations myself. Certainly I was not eager to believe in the truth of my dreams of UFO abduction, or even to take literally the dozens of hours of careful hypnotic retrieval of those terrible ordeals. Even when I came to understand that these memories were largely accurate, were not fantasies or confabulations, or masks for childhood sexual abuse, I resisted the message of the Harvesters. Who wants to face the dismal fact that human life is meaningless? What kind of stoical stalwart can deal, day after bleak day, with the awful news that we all—child and adult, felon and saint—have no more significance in the darkly radiant scheme of spiritual evolution than... what? A snake's discarded husk? A male spider chomped by his female mate after his small spasm has inseminated her?

Worse: than the severed placenta thrown carelessly into a hospital bucket after the bloody labors of birth?

But it is so. I must not hide the truth from you, or from myself.

We are of no more significance in the real universe, the invisible, impalpable immensity of dark matter that comprises the true cosmos, than a lump of bloody afterbirth.

But of course, that is only true from the narrow perspective of our puffed human pretensions. A placenta, after all, however lowly and disposable, is not without meaning to the child it nourishes for nine months in the womb. The growing snake's skin has protected it for a season, before it splits into tatters and is left by the side of the road. A baby's first teeth loosen and fall out within a very few years, and for a day we treasure them whimsically, placing them beneath the child's pillow and promising that a fairy will bear them away to some finer land. We pay our gappy infants in good coin for the privilege. As we tuck a dollar bill beneath the pillow, and whisk the milk tooth into the trash, we do not despise that small fragment of organic detritus. But we do not believe our fairytale, either.

The meaning of the lost tooth is not salvation in a heaven of tooth fairies, it is the adult dentition that springs up to fill its gap. And the meaning of terrestrial life is not a transcendental afterlife for the dying human—starving child or withered sage, automobile accident victim or cancer patient, AIDS patient or his selfless helper. The meaning of human life is not afterlife but afterbirth: we are a disposable stage in the production of the Children of Heaven, our Scions, the first casts, the happy miscarriages, the uncorrupted abortions. Those who perish in the flesh before crude matter has infected, corrupted and swiftly corroded their potentially immortal souls. Little wonder that all the false religions of pomp and human glory, intellectual and fundamentalist alike, denounce abortion as the vilest sin. No. Far from being a sin, a crime, an atrocity, it is the release of our Scions into eternity, and so, even as the churchmen pretend to squabble among themselves, they conspire wickedly to prevent this sacrament, this single good deed of human flesh, this midwifery of heaven.

ix.

Three days after his outrageous revelation, on a gorgeous Californian summer's day, Benjamin picked me up in his black retro-fitted Porche 944 Turbo and drove me to my father's West Coast home in Malibu.

I was all of a dither, as you will understand, but I did what I could to hide my emotions. This was easily enough done, given my childhood conditioning, but I also wished to avoid slipping into some disabling multiple personality confusion, so I gave vent to my mixed feelings by squeezing my wide brimmed ozone hat in my hands until its sturdy genetically engineered cotton was crushed into a shapeless lump. Benjamin certainly noticed these small convulsions but, adroit therapist that he was (and is), he refrained from comment.

"Did you get the book I sent over?"

I had been studying the yellowed pages of *The Dying Breed* all morning. None of the photos was labeled, so I could not even be sure if Margaret was included. One woman poised on top of an old automobile, haughty and proud, bore a certain resemblance to the face I saw in the mirror, when I could bear to look in the mirror. Still, it had given me a curious and visceral thrill to see her name on the dedication page, placed there by the man who was allegedly my father. And there was a suite of portraits of babies viewed through glass, rows and ranks of the tiny wrinkled things, big pink heads and squinty eyes, and a wry nurse standing to one side of a complex bit of machinery sustaining a tiny little creature barely alive by the look of it. I had a terrible feeling that one was me.

"Yes, thank you. Yes, thank you. The courier service is more reliable than the damned post office." The mail had never recovered after the 9/11 terrorism horrors. and the competition from email.

"Have a look at these," Benjamin said, and passed me a folio. He was a handsome man of 45, more boyish than distinguished, and I trusted him implicitly, which is more than I'd been able to do with anyone else since the day I'd escaped from the cult. The photographs were in a variety of styles and voices. I peered out, two or three years old, in big eyed fascination from some of them, or painted colorful daubs with my fingers, or stuffed food into my mouth, laughing and happy. This time I recognized myself at once, and my adult eyes burned with misery and loss. I turned the sheets slowly, examining each hungrily. The first convincing shot of Margaret caused me to utter a soft cry, a hand squeezed at my diaphragm, for it was me staring back at myself: an offbeat beauty, if one made allowances for her awful seventies" haircut and make-up and clothes: defended, waspishly amused. They had burned all her photos at Harmony, of course. Restrained by my seat belt, I leaned forward in the urban racing seat to hug the picture to me, eyes prickling, breathing in little gasps.

X.

The Reverend Daimon Keith lived in ecologically responsible luxury. Behind a high fence laced with sensors and lethal devices, his marvelous house, designed according to principles allegedly revealed by UFO architects but thought to resemble certain embargoed ideas from blockaded Saudi, sucked at the sun and polluted air like a flower and turned it into a cool, faintly rose-scented breeze, gentle indirect lighting, and full-surround musical background. I walked into a round white room carpeted in pale green, with startling art works suspended on the walls: thick slabs of wood in bright gold and purple and crimson, curves and arcs above and radiating bars below, Samuel Barber's exquisite Violin Concerto entering its second movement and tearing my heart out as it did so, and my father, clad for the occasion in normal business suit, having forsaken his silver flying saucer garment or rainbow robes, standing up to greet me from a sunken pit in the center of the room. His throat worked visibly, and he swayed, and to my astonishment and immense gratification he burst into tears.

"Jesus," he blurted. "Margaret!" Then he shook his head, squeezed his eyes shut, came toward me like a man dazed. "I'm sorry, Flake. Oh God."

We went into each other's arms as if we had never been separated, and everything went very runny and snotty for a while.

xi.

Daimon flew me to Sydney, where his wife Zelda preferred to live, and we walked along Bondi Beach while a pair of inconspicuous Scionetics heavies paced us for our own protection. Somehow the Australians had managed to clean up the foreshore with its wonderful white sand, and depollute the blue and white surf, which had been turning into a sewer, Deems told me, last time I'd been here with my murdered mother. We rolled up our trouser legs and splashed at the edge of the mild winter sea.

"I don't understand any of it," I told him, holding his hand. By rights, according to the symptomatology of my condition, I should not have been able to bear his touch, or anyone's.

Alternatively, I should have been hard at the task of seducing him with glancing laughing eyes and hints of cleavage, all that. Somehow, though, wonderfully, this was, for the moment at least, simply homecoming. I was all wept out by that point, and my heart was torn two ways at once: by uncomplex happiness and by a more profound dull emptiness that made mockery of the happiness. "What does it mean?" I asked my father, who had made hundreds of millions of dollars and bought the huge old building up on the top of the bluff by telling hundreds of thousands of desperate people his awful answer to that question.

"Come on," he said, "let's get some fish and chips."

We bought piping hot fried shark in batter—it is called "flake" in Australia, which made us both laugh—and french fries ("chips"), and a six-pack of lite beer to wash it down with. One of the heavies fetched a thick woven blanket so we could sit on the sand without getting piles, my father said, wincing at some memory, and a pair of light, insulated capes to keep the breeze at bay. Daimon tore open the paper bag of french fries and inhaled the dietetically dubious odor of salt and vinegar.

"The meaning of it all? Darling, let me tell you what I've learned, what the grays have taught me. You won't enjoy hearing this, but it will," he said seriously, "set you free."

I was apprehensive.

"You're going to say that human life has no meaning," I told him. I knew already that this was his scandalous doctrine, because I had gobbled up a couple of potted and scathing magazine exposes of Scionetics in the previous days, and I wasn't buying it.

He popped the top on a beer can (a "stubby") and sucked froth into his mouth. The sun, burning down from the north of the sky, caught his machine-tanned forehead, slipped down the laugh lines beside his eyes. He should have been wearing a hat, of course, as I was, because the ozone hole was straight overhead in Sydney, but he was protected against cancer, he said, by the painful ministrations of the Harvesters.

"No meaning? Not exactly," he said. "Look, Flake—hey, you

don't mind me calling you that, do you?"

I smiled primly. "Not so long as you share *that* flake with me."

He tore me off a hot fat piece of fish, wrapped one end in a double thickness of paper to save my fingers, and passed it over.

"All right, Flake, can you sit still for my two minute lecture on the meaning of meaning?"

I shrugged, nibbling shark. It was sweet and delicious.

"Okay, the starting point is that everyone gets everything arse backwards because they're always facing the wrong way. I mean the philosophers, the theologians, the anthropocists, the fucking quantum holists, everyone except for a handful of old-fashioned semioticians. And even they squibbed when it came to the jump."

"Oh dear." I pushed back the brim of my hat and gazed across the Pacific ocean. Sea gulls circled, trying to snatch our fries. "Sorry, this reminds me of Valentine and the great truth of Harmonic Resonance." The comparison, risen unbidden, made me shudder. Deems watched me. He did not put his arm around me, which was wise at that moment.

"Yes," he said, "we all think we're the first and only ones to understand the secret of the universe. I was always suspicious of people who thought they knew it all. I loved to take the mickey out of the bastards." He sighed. "I'd still be running about like a perpetual adolescent if the Harvesters hadn't told me what's what."

"And what *is* what?"

A lolloping dog ran past, spraying us with sand. I threw him a cooling chip, and he missed it. What was his notion of the good life? This, surely. And what did his doggy mind imagine was the meaning of the world? But we were not doggies. We made our own chips and beer and polluted our own beaches and cleaned them up if we felt like it.

"Look at the words we use when we ask the most poignant questions, Flake," my father said. "When your mother abducted you and ran off to the States, I raved and flailed and ranted.

Why? I screamed. Why did this happen to me? I flew to America and tried to find you, and nobody would tell me, and then the fucking guru went to ground with all his witless devotees, taking you and your mother with him, and I had to come back to Australia, and then I was snatched for three weeks by the Harvesters— Christ, it sounds like a bloody soap opera! Well, I ranted and flailed, when they brought me back, and spent a lot of time screaming, *Why*? And when your mother was killed and they told you she'd died in a car crash, you probably ran about asking Why, why, why?"

"I was five years old," I told Deems. "Of course I did."

"Okay, what's the common element here? Three different strokes of ill fortune, and we keeping asking Why? But that's a question that is only appropriately addressed to an intention. Do you see what I mean? Why had Margaret stolen you to America? I've thought about this a lot, Angel—"

"Rosa," I said.

He gulped, and his eyes misted.

"Rosa, I was a typical male of my era. Well, not typical, but even so. And your mother was a confused but strong woman, and she wasn't going to put up with my bullshit. Of course she had to go away. It wasn't me, precisely—it was all of us, our stupid culture, the way we find meaning in attachment to our kids.... She thought Zelda and I were stealing you away from her, and she was probably right."

"I don't even remember Zelda," I said in a grainy tone.

"You'll meet her tonight, she's looking forward enormously to seeing you. But the point is, I wasn't asking for those sorts of answers. I wanted to know Why is the universe doing this to me? Why has the plan of my life—the central plan of the universe, after all—why has it gone so unfairly off the rails? I'm the hero of this fucking movie, right? How dare the extras screw with my happy ending?"

"I suppose we all put ourself in the main role," I conceded, because that's what he wanted me to agree to. But I didn't, not really. My response to disappointment and pain and, indeed, intolerable torment had been to shrink myself, to split my soul into the colors of the rainbow and hide most of the hues in darkness. That's why I've been able to construct this history of my father and my mother and myself, don't you see? I'm the perfect biographer. I have no self. I'm anyone's. I'm anyone.

"Actors spend a lot of time obsessing about Why questions," Deems said. "Motivation. 'What's my character's motivation?' They're looking for a few simple codes, cues to the impulses and behavioral channels of the personality they're about to impersonate. And it's not so strange or hard to do that, because evolution built our brains to perform exactly that function. It's why people love stories."

"We've evolved to be actors?" I stared at him. "I think you've been living in Los Angeles too long."

Deems laughed gustily. "You're Margaret's daughter all right." We both stared at the horizon for a time. "If you're a horse," he said then, patiently, "your DNA built you to graze in a herd, and avoid lions. If you're a lion, your DNA built you to hunt horses in the company of a small squadron of other lions. In both cases, you need an internal model of social life—your own, and your prey's or predator's. When a horse sees the grass sway, it's a considerable benefit if she asks herself horsily, Why did that happen? What's its meaning? Lion or wind? Sniff sniff. Freak, shit, Lion! Lion! Meaning starts by interpreting as deliberate codes the lumpy happenstances of the world."

I mused on this. "It's the other way round, isn't it? We interpret the meaning that's there. I mean, if a Chinese translator interprets my words from English, she's got to start by understanding my meaning and sort of...carry it over to the other language?"

"Okay, both processes entail each other. The grass means food to our horsie, and its motion might mean danger, because our horsie means food to the lions. So the nutritive values and the possibility of lions are both there in the grass, I guess, before any act of interpretation takes place. But you can't say they have any meaning, in that exact sense, unless the horse is there to start with. Meaning is not pre-existent; it emerges."

Some Aussie bravos were taking to the frothy water in gaudy wetsuits, clambering on to windsurfers. We watched their antics. Their play was as meaningless, as arbitrary, as open to an inpouring of significance as a whale sounding, as the Budd Hopkins Guardians on my father's Los Angeles' walls. For the surfers, its meaning was the joy of sinew and muscle and eye doing their stuff, the body's balance sustained against the chaotic turbulence of the sea. I sighed.

"I mentioned two other cases," Deems said. "My three-week abduction, and your mother's death. Why did they happen? What was the meaning?"

I sent him a sidelong glance. "Well, I don't even know if it did happen. Your disappearance. Sorry."

He gazed back without expression. "It doesn't matter, you see. Call it a metaphor, if you like."

I was relieved. "All right."

"The answer is, there is no meaning to either event—in the usual, human-centered sense. Something happens, okay. A tree falls over in the forest. All sorts of factors led up to that event— the rain has weakened the soil, the tree's DNA program has closed down its growth cycle so it's gone rotten inside, the wind has picked up because of the accidental arrangement of snow and cloud halfway around the world. So it's all explicable, down to the level of atoms if you had time enough to track it all. But it's not part of any plan. And if you happen to be walking under the tree at that moment and it squashes you flat, all we can say is—'shit happens'."

"Or: don't walk under trees. That might be one meaning."

"A meaning we read into the sad event, sure. We don't draw it out, we put it in. That's what our brains are good at—making up stories, scripts, schemata. The cognitive scientists have a whole batch of words for this stuff. All of it boils down to one hard fact: we love to write the universe into a text, and then to interpret it as if someone else had written it. That's okay. Horses do it, lions do it, the birds and bees do it." He grinned wickedly.

"It's only when we start to fetishize our little knack that it goes crazy and cancerous and eats us up from the inside. We start *looking* for meaning everywhere, forgetting that *we're* the ones who *put* it there."

It was getting chilly, and I felt sorry for those guys out there on their windsurfers. But then nobody was forcing them to do it. We stood up and stretched, shook sand off the blanket by holding one corner of it each, handed the folded bundle to one of Daimon's patient bodyguards who took it back to the car. In the froth at the edge of the sea I noticed two or three limp, diaphanous jellyfish. I bent down to stir them with my finger, and drew back in disgust. They were condoms, washing about in the sandy foam.

"Daimon, this sounds like the crappy New Age solipsism I grew up with. 'You create your own universe.' I'm sorry, but that's the worst kind of hypocrisy."

"No, no," my father said placidly, placing his big-toed feet carefully in someone else's line of footsteps in the sand. He had to hop a little. "All we create is our own meaning. The world, other people, our own inaccessible inward systems—all of that provides the building materials, and the landscape for the architect to work in. But the meaning we end up with is a construct of our minds. It has no necessary connection to the actual priorities of the universe."

"Which are?"

He laughed softly. "Which have nothing to do with us, I'm sorry to say."

"With us human beings? Benjamin said you don't believe people have souls. Is that what he meant?"

"We *produce* souls," my father said. "Cows produce methane when they fart, and destroy the ozone layer. Radioactive decay deep inside the Earth produces thermal plumes that cause volcanoes. We produce fetuses with souls. If they're lucky, they die in time. Or the gray doctors come down and harvest them."

I heard all this with the greatest disquiet, understanding none of it yet. It was too soon, and luckily Deems changed the topic to my own life, the confused and miserable tale of my tragical history with and without my mother.

xii.

Later we drove up to the great house when Zelda lived, and I met the rest of my family. My step-mother looked pretty good for a woman nearing seventy. They gave me a fine guest room overlooking the sea, and I slept with the window open for the first time in years. Waves hushed at the foot of the cliff. I dreamed of condoms, and small things squirming, and woke screaming in the strange space of the room.

xiii.

A month later, Deems had vanished again. He hasn't come back. His devotees assure me that he has been taken to some finer realm—Mars, perhaps, where he thought his visage had been shaped like an icon gazing at the stars, or the center of the Earth, or to some alternative dimension. How can I know what to believe? Does it matter? There is no text of the universe outside our inscription of its glyphs, and no meaning beyond our free interpretation. My father, true to his own analysis, or perhaps flying in its face, affected to despise biographies, to detest movies and novels and stories of every kind. "Fiction is the gossip of those who don't get out much, Rosa," he told me, a week before he disappeared, "purveyed by those who don't get out at all." Whether or not we have souls and an afterlife is the kind of question, perhaps the kind of fiction, one should abandon at the departure lounge into adulthood, I now see. I live a quiet life of satisfactory despair. Sometimes I dream of my mother, but just as often I confuse her with Katie, recalling only Mom's heavy Southern drawl. Zelda and I run the household, hardly an arduous duty, waiting for Daimon's return, and the Scionetics heavies grow more bizarre with each year but dutifully top up our swollen bank accounts. Benjamin and I have two healthy babies. Neither of them, to the best of our knowledge, has been abducted by the Harvesters. I float in the huge tub, scrubbing at my pale flesh, and dream of great dark eyes in pale swollen skulls, and tell myself again and again the story of Deems and Margaret and my beloved Benjamin and all the sweet burdens of time.

xiv.

The Starseed Signals received by Dr. Leary and Wayne Benner in Folsom Prison, in July-August, 1973, tell us that it is time for "life on Earth to leave the planetary womb and learn to walk through the stars." Life on this planet is now at the halfway point, having produced "nervous systems capable of communicating with and returning to the Galactic Network" where our Interstellar Parents await us. Mankind is about to discover "the key to immortality in the chemical structure of the genetic code.. the scripture of life." At this time, the signals invite us, the "voyage home is possible.... Mutate! Come home in glory."
Brad Steiger, *The Gods of Aquarius: UFOs and the Transformation of Man*, 1976

He hovers, curled in upon himself like a great balding, wrinkled fetus. It's the usual hazy nowhere under pale ribbed metal. Cupped by buoyancy, rocking airborne above dull convexity, he dreams his lucid dreams. All the cycles of metabolism flow as before, his chest expands and contracts in the mechanical bellows of breath. At the edge of awareness, hiding or at least refusing to disclose themselves there in the shadows, the gray Harvesters peer with their unblinking gaze. All about and through him is the humming rapid motion of a billion molecular probes at his trillion synapses. Without waking, without sleeping, he is aware of this prosaic violation.

"Take me back," he tells them through lips too heavy to open. His voice is blurred and hopelessly distorted, lost in the anechoic void, but he knows that they hear him by other than vocal means.

Klar-2 speaks to him through dark wraparound eyes. You must stay with us this time. We will take you to a city all of gold, where the leaves of the tree are for the healing of all nations.

"Horseshit," my father says, forcing his lips to shape the syllables.

Behold, a pale horse, the gray doctor tells him without the slightest trace of humor: and his name that sat on him was Death.

Deems is shown the customary storm of visions. The world is consumed in nuclear fire. Great chasms open in its soft, ripened skin, and all the numbers of humankind tumble into the burning depths. Air sours, foully poisoned, an acid-rain storm that blights every flowering plant and tree and crop in the world. Maggots eat at lambs and babies. Transparent demons move like wraiths at the center of the earth among the last of the living, tormenting them eternally. It is a terrifying spectacle, disturbing as a nightmare one cannot awaken from. But Deems has been this way before. He is too frightened to laugh, but it is preposterous. This has to be the unadulterated noise of the unconscious, the cheese sandwich he ate before turning in, a mask or screen for something else.

"Pull the other one," he croaks, "it has bells on it."

A little girl comes forward, thin as a Bosnian refugee, pale and gaunt, limbs like a foal's. Her hair is thin and straggly, and she looks at him without fear or expectation.

Take her in your arms, Klar-2 tells him. Give her your human warmth. Kindle her into life. This is your daughter.

"Why do you have doorways and ramps if you can take us through walls and fly us in the air," skeptical Deems insists, exhausted and scratchy. "Why must you torment us with crude surgery when a painless scraping of cells from the inside of the mouth could give you more genetic material than you'd ever need? After all this time, Christ, two thousand years, ten thousand, why are you still tampering with our poor bodies? If you can calm us and heal our hurt, why do you continue to bring such torment to your victims? If we have no souls, why do you terrify simple village children with visions of eternal damnation?"

His throat is dry, hoarse, and the mouse dropping stench is making him feel sick. He tries to turn his head, to look Klar-2 and the others straight in the eye, and they stir uneasily and shift like shadows, like candle smoke in the candle flame's heat.

The little hybrid child gazes at him, arms hanging desolate at her sides. She wears a kind of white shift, and her limbs are painfully thin.

He struggles in the air, struggles for purchase on nothingness, with immense effort brings his heavy feet over the edge of the operating table and down to the tepid warmth of the floor. They rustle and move aside, withdrawing into the shadows, into the light. The girl child stands dumbly, fatherless, motherless, aching, alien, human.

Daimon Keith, my father, reaches out his own arms, then, at last, and enfolds me within them.

ACKNOWLEDGMENTS

"Time Considered as a Series of Thermite Burns in No Particular Order" was first published at Tor.com, May, 2011. Copyright © 2011 by Damien Broderick.

"All Summer Long" (as "Serf") was first published in *Winners Are Grinners,* ed. by Paul Collins and Meredith Costain, Pearson, 2000. Copyright © 2000 by Damien Broderick.

"The Beancounter's Cat" was first published in *Eclipse Four,* ed. by Jonathan Strahan, Nightshade Books, 2011. Copyright © 2011 by Damien Broderick.

"Under the Moons of Venus" was first published in *Subterranean*, ed. by Jonathan Strahan, Spring, 2010. Copyright © 2010 by Damien Broderick.

"Luminous Fish" by Damien Broderick and Paul Di Filippo appears here for the first time. Copyright © 2012 by Damien Broderick and Paul Di Filippo.

"Coming Back" was first published in *The Magazine of Fantasy & Science Fiction,* December, 1982. Copyright © 1982 by Damien Broderick.

"Walls of Flesh, Bars of Bone" by Damien Broderick and Barbara Lamar was first published in *Engineering Infinity,* ed. by Jonathan Strahan, 2010. Copyright © 2010 by Damien Broderick and Barbara Lamar.

"All My Yesterdays" was first published in *Chaos*, 1964, and revised slightly in *Glass Reptile Breakout,* ed. by Van Ikin, Center for Studies in Australian Literature, 1990. Copyright © 1964, 1990 by Damien Broderick.

ABOUT THE AUTHOR

DAMIEN BRODERICK is an Australian science fiction and popular science writer. He lives in San Antonio, Texas, with his wife, tax attorney Barbara Lamar.

Five of Broderick's books have won Ditmar Awards; the first, *The Dreaming Dragons*, was runner-up for the John W. Campbell Memorial Award for Best Science Fiction Novel, and was listed in David Pringle's *Science Fiction: The 101 Best Novels, 1949-1984*. He has also won the Aurealis award four times. In November 2003, Broderick was awarded a grant for 2004-05 by the Australia Council to write fiction exploring the technological singularity. In 2005 he received the Distinguished Scholarship Award of the International Association for the Fantastic in the Arts. In 2010 and 2011, he was a finalist in the juried Theodore Sturgeon Award for best sf short story of the preceding year, and at the World Science Fiction Convention received the A. Bertram Chandler Memorial Award for 2010.

His science fiction novel *The Judas Mandala* is credited with the first appearance of the term "virtual reality," and his 1997 popular science book *The Spike* was the first to investigate the technological Singularity in detail.

Broderick holds a Ph.D. in Literary Studies from Deakin University, Australia, with a dissertation relating to the comparative semiotics of scientific, literary, and science fictional textuality. In 2012, he published *Science Fiction: The 101 Best Novels, 1985-2010,* the successor to Pringle's famous survey, co-authored with Paul Di Filippo.